A
FAMILIAR
PROBLEM

STEVEN D. BREWER

A
FAMILIAR
PROBLEM

1

A FAMILIAR START

RORY BITTERLY KICKED A STONE off the sidewalk as he left the Throckmorton Magical Academy and headed home in the late afternoon. He was thoroughly disgusted with himself and shook his mop of blond hair angrily.

The other students were all excited about choosing a familiar and some had already selected one. But Rory hadn't found the right one yet. He didn't want something trite, like a cat. Or stupid, like a bird. Or ugly, like a toad. It had to be cool. And powerful. And when he'd tried to explain himself, he'd come off sounding like some kind of arrogant jerk. Or maybe just a fool. And all the other students had laughed at him.

He really wanted to learn battle magic. He could do a pretty good shield already. He'd even taught himself one offensive spell—which was against the rules for students to actually use outside of class. To support him, he wanted a familiar that could be an ally in a fight. Oh, sure! A cat or bird could offer useful intelligence, but they couldn't really fight alongside you. And that was what he dreamed of—what he wanted more than anything.

He walked down the hill. After waiting for a cargo cart to pass, he crossed the street and turned right at the corner store. Further down the street, he saw some children arranged in a circle around a cardboard box. As he got closer, he could see that the box had a sign on it that said FREE and the kids were reaching into the box to touch something.

"Aren't they cute?" a brown girl in a pink dress said.

"I think I'll take this one," a tow-headed boy said.

"My parents won't let me have one," a Black girl said.

Rory looked in the box and saw four little kittens. One was white, two were tiger-striped, and the last was all black with bright, yellow eyes.

In a moment, all of the kittens were taken but the black one.

"Don't take the cursed one," the tow-headed boy said.

"That's just an old wives' tale," the girl in the pink dress said.

"No, it's not," another boy with black hair insisted. "Black cats are evil. We should kill it."

Rory couldn't believe his ears. The boy picked up a rock and Rory placed himself between him and the box.

"It's just a little kitten," he said. "It's not evil."

"It's getting away!" the other girl said.

Rory spun and saw that the kitten had jumped out of the box and was darting down the sidewalk. The black-haired boy drew back his arm to throw the rock and Rory sprinted after the cat. He scooped up the kitten just as a rock struck the spot on the sidewalk. And then he was being pelted with rocks. One hit him in the shoulder and another on the leg.

Rory spoke a word of power and brought up his shield. Although it did not stop the rocks entirely, it reduced their velocity enough that they didn't hurt. Then he jumped off the sidewalk, skidded down a little slope into the park, and hightailed it through the playground. He stopped at the pavilion beyond that lay next to the creek.

He dropped his shield and rubbed his bruises. His skin was an unhealthy pale color because he'd been out so little in the year since his mom died and the bruises were already turning an ugly purple. He looked at the kitten. It looked back at him with bright, yellow eyes.

"You sure are trouble," he said.

The kitten licked its paws and wiped its face.

"Maybe I ought to name you," he said. "But I don't know if you're a girl kitten or a boy kitten."

The kitten seemingly paid him no mind. Despite that, Rory had this odd feeling he couldn't shake that he was being watched. Well, not watched exactly: It felt more like being studied, or scrutinized, under a magnifying glass like a specimen.

"I wonder if you'd like some milk ..." he said. He knew you shouldn't give kittens too much milk, but he figured a little was probably okay.

He bought a small bottle of milk at the concession stand under the pavilion. He opened the lid, poured a little bit into the lid, and set it on the ground. He then placed the kitten down next to the lid to see what it might do.

The kitten sniffed the milk then began to lap it up from the lid. Although it was a small act, he still felt an absurd pleasure as he watched the tiny creature. For just a moment, he considered making the kitten his familiar. Still, he couldn't get past the inescapable fact that cats were incredibly trite as familiars. He resolved again to find something better.

He gave the kitten a little more before drinking the rest himself.

After finishing the milk, the kitten chased its tail and then began to pounce on ants on the sidewalk. He watched it with amusement, until it spotted a damselfly, pounced on it, but missed and fell into the river.

He surged to his feet to see it thrashing in the water as it was swept down the stream. He raced around, jumped a fence, and got ahead of it. He waded out into the chilly water as the flow carried it to him. As fast as he could, he plucked the kitten out of the water. The poor thing seemed half drowned, but it was alive. He tucked it inside his shirt to dry it off and keep it warm.

"A LOT of trouble," he said, amplifying his earlier words to the kitten. He felt a weird little jolt of pleasure that seemed to come out of nowhere.

After his daring rescue, he was already closer to the far side of the river, so he simply waded the rest of the way across.

Taking stock of which way was home, he decided the fastest way was through the woods. Otherwise, it would mean a lengthy detour to one of the two bridges to get back to the sidewalk, or another trip through the river. Given the waterlogged state of his shoes, he opted to squelch his way over to a trail that would lead him straight through the woods toward home.

He reached the edge of the forest and followed the trail under the boughs of the great trees. As he moved deeper into the forest, it got darker and darker. Wild elementals were visible here and there through the darkness. He hadn't realized how low the sun had already gotten. Back in the playground, it was still pretty bright and the elemental lights hadn't yet come on, but under the trees, it was becoming hard to see. The trail, however, was smooth, clearly marked, and easy to follow—although it was still a bit scary to have it be so dark.

As though responding to his fear, something howled. It was still a ways off, but it was a blood-curdling sound. He'd never heard anything like it before. He picked up his pace and began to walk more quickly. Then it howled again. And this time, it was much closer.

He saw something—eyes—glowing up ahead in the trail, coming toward him.

He spoke the word of power to bring up his shield again. In the dim light, it was visible as a slightly-blue glow limning his body. The glowing eyes got closer and the creature emerged from the gloom: a direwolf.

He had no idea what a direwolf was doing in a town park. He'd thought they were the sort of thing you only found in remote and distant lands. But he knew one when he saw one and this was unquestionably a direwolf. What was it even doing here?

He prepared to cast a fireball. Although students weren't supposed to use offensive magic, he decided that now was not the time to be worried about something like that.

The direwolf crept forward and then sprang. He spoke the word of power, his shield dropped, but a grapefruit-sized fireball appeared and splashed over the direwolf, making it yelp and blasting it backwards into the woods.

He turned and started sprinting hoping he could reach the far side of the forest before the direwolf recovered. But he had been running for no more than a minute when it sprang on him from behind and knocked him down. He twisted so he wouldn't land on the kitten, but his shirt slipped open and the kitten spilled out onto the trail. The direwolf bypassed him and grabbed the kitten, shaking it viciously like a toy and throwing it to the side.

"No!" he screamed. He ran to the kitten that was lying bloodied and still by the side of the trail.

Standing over the tiny kitten, he spun, and filled with righteous rage, he spoke another word of power and unleashed another fireball. But this time, he poured all his anger and fury into the spell and produced a beach ball-sized fireball that blazed like the sun in the dark forest.

The direwolf couldn't avoid the fireball and was engulfed in flames. It thrashed wildly, yelping, then fell over and was still. But Rory had already turned his attention to the tiny kitten.

"Oh, no. Oh, no. Oh, no," he said over and over again, picking up the tiny kitten. In the dark, he couldn't even tell if it was still breathing. He choked up and began to cry.

The next thing he knew, he found himself lying on his back with a naked, very dark-skinned woman astride his body. He was momentarily mesmerized by her large, out-thrust breasts. She put a finger under his chin to force him to look up at her face and her bright, yellow cat eyes. In the darkness, her vertical pupils were fully open. She had a wild mane of thick, wiry black hair. She brought her face close to his and licked his tears with a rough tongue.

"Aww, you're so sweet!" she purred. "You'll do."

"You … You're not a cat," he said.

"That's right."

"It was after you, not me," he said, putting it together.

"Right again," she said, licking her lips. "Or, rather, it was sent."

"What are you?"

"I'm a demon. I've been looking for someone like you."

"Are you … Do you want to be my familiar?" he asked.

"Oh, no," she said. "You're going to be mine."

She gestured at his throat and a translucent collar materialized around his neck with a shining cord that she held in her fist.

"Are you ready?" she asked.

"For what?"

"Direwolves always hunt in packs, Sugar," she said, springing up and pulling him to his feet. And, as if on cue, a chorus of howls broke out all around them.

Rory saw three pairs of eyes closing in from two sides.

"You take the one on the left. I'll take the two on the right."

Then, before he could move, she grabbed his face between her hands and gave him a long, deep kiss, thrusting her rough tongue into his mouth.

"For luck!"

He brought up his shield again. This time, it blazed white around him.

He turned to face the direwolf, then started to reach deep down deep inside himself trying to find the same kind of energy he'd been able to find before. But he found he was already overflowing with power. It was like he was so full it was sloshing out over the top. The direwolves sprang as one. He spoke the word of power, his shield dropped again, but this time a gigantic fireball, nearly his height in diameter, incinerated the direwolf and then kept going. It knocked down a whole row of trees in the forest, scattering sparks everywhere, and eventually spent itself leaving a glassy depression in the distant hillside.

He stood for a long moment, stunned, as the afterimages faded from his vision, listening to crash after crash as trees fell onto other trees and branches dropped. And then there was silence.

He spun to check on the demon. She was licking blood off her right hand, standing over the corpses of the other direwolves that had their throats torn out.

She patted him on the head with her unbloodied left hand, then twirled a lock of his unruly hair around her finger.

"Good boy!" she said. "Here's your reward." And she pulled him into an embrace and forcefully kissed him again. He could taste the coppery, salty blood on her lips and rough tongue. He was unsettled for a second, but after only the briefest moment of reflection, he decided this was something he could get used to. He relaxed, closed his eyes, and leaned into her.

"Don't forget that you're my familiar!" she said, lifting her hand and the translucent glowing cord that led to the collar around his neck revealed itself again. Then in a flash, the collar and cord vanished and he found himself with a kitten in his arms. She rubbed her head on him, marking him and purring.

He walked the rest of the way home, his head swimming with confusion and questions. What had just happened? Was he going crazy? What did it mean? What even were demons? And why would a demon want him for a familiar?

When he got home, he went straight to the living room to talk to his dad.

"Oh, did you finally choose a familiar?" his dad asked. "I thought you didn't want a cat ..."

"It's ... It's kind of a long story," he said, dodging the question. "Can I keep her?"

"You shouldn't assume it's female just because it's a cat. Are you even sure it's a girl?"

"Oh, I'm pretty sure," Rory said.

2

AN UNFAMILIAR NAME
(100 TRALONGS)

Rory didn't get back home again until late in the evening. After allowing him to keep the kitten, his father had directed him to go and, using nearly all of his saved money, to purchase the necessary supplies for keeping a cat. He entered the dark house and found his father had already gone to bed. He gestured with intention and the elemental lights came on in the kitchen.

Rory pulled out his purchases. He set out a water dish and a food dish in the kitchen. He opened a small can of kitten food and put it into the dish and set it on the floor. The pet bed went in his bedroom. He grabbed the litter box and a package of litter and carried them across the hall to the bathroom. He reached out to open the door when it popped open and she was standing there, in human form, naked, looking at him with her bright, yellow eyes. He nearly screamed in shock but managed to stifle it into a grunt.

"I guess you don't really need this," he said.

"You should put it out anyway," she said. "It will aid with the deception we are practicing."

He set the litter box behind the door and filled it with the package of kitty litter.

"You don't need to put out any food either," she said. "I don't need to eat. And I certainly don't need to eat *that*."

"You don't need to eat? At all? But you can eat? Is there anything you like to eat?" he asked.

"Meat!" she said, smiling broadly and showing her teeth.

"That figures," he said, rolling his eyes.

He brushed his teeth and used the bathroom before returning to his bedroom. She had returned to kitten form and was lying curled up on the pet bed. He considered petting her, but decided that was too weird, so he just got into bed by himself. After the excitement of the day, he fell asleep quickly and slept deeply. But he had weird dreams. He dreamed he was looking through a photo album with pictures of his childhood with big yellow eyes looking over his shoulder.

He awoke groggily before dawn. He smelled something sweet and felt something warm and soft touching his lips. There was something deeply nostalgic about the odor, but in his somnolent state he couldn't quite put his finger on it.

"Would you like some nummies?" she said, rubbing her nipple on his mouth. Still half asleep, he latched on to her nipple and suddenly his throat was flooded with warm, sweet milk. He swallowed and, as fast as he could gulp, his mouth was filled with milk.

When the first breast was emptied, she slipped a finger in his mouth to break his latch, then shifted slightly to put her other breast in his mouth. He nursed eagerly on that breast as well. Once it was emptied, she broke his latch again.

"It's time for you to get up, Sugar," she said. He opened his eyes and looked up at her, his head filled with confusing, warring emotions. She looked right back at him with her bright, yellow eyes.

"What's happening?" he asked. "What are you doing to me?"

"I'm just waking you up, Sugar," she said. "You need to start your training."

"Training?"

"Yes," she said. "I'm going to be training you extensively. Physical fitness, martial arts, and advanced offensive and defensive magical techniques."

His eyes got big.

"Really?" he asked. She nodded. He bounced out of bed. "I'm ready! Let's get started!"

"Let's start with having you go for a run. See how far you can go today by yourself. Then, tomorrow, we'll see how far you can run with me … encouraging you," she said, patting his head. "And do your best. I'll know if you don't."

He dressed, putting on shorts, a shirt, and his running shoes.

"One more thing, Sugar," the demon said, reclining in his bed, watching him. "You're doing fine right now. But never forget that, although punishment is generally counterproductive, I will punish you if you ever persist in being disobedient. Do you understand?"

He nodded, then turned and headed out into the crisp, pre-dawn air. He paused at the street trying to decide which way to go. After a moment, he decided to run to the graveyard where his mom was buried.

He walked for a block to stretch his legs and warm up, then set off at a comfortable trot. He passed the houses of his neighborhood, then reached the larger road and followed that through town. He went by the town green and the great chestnut tree that was a town landmark.

Rory was glad to be out early. The sidewalks were mostly empty at this hour, although the streets were full of the cargo carts that had arrived via the Blink Network overnight and were being taken to their final destinations. Soon, however, the sidewalks would be jammed with commuters like his dad, walking to use the Blink Network to head to their jobs.

At the far outskirts, he ran down the steep hill into the valley that formed the northern boundary of the town. After crossing the bridge over the river in the valley, he ran up the other side until he ran out of breath. He walked up the last hundred yards until he reached the top then picked up his pace again. He took the right into the graveyard and followed the path toward the right as it curved around to the very end. Near the back of the graveyard, he paused.

His mom only had a small marker. It was in a nice spot, however, that had a beautiful view looking east where the valley turned to the north. The sun was just rising when he arrived, his breath steaming in the cool air.

"Hi, Mom," Rory said. "You'll never believe what's happened. You know how I couldn't find a familiar? Well, I still didn't find one. But something else happened and it might be even better."

He got an odd feeling, like he was being watched and he remembered what the demon had said. So, after another minute, he started running again. He pushed on the rest of the way through the graveyard and then retraced his steps home. He tried to pick up the pace a bit, though he still had to walk up the last little bit of the climb out of the valley. And he arrived home winded and sweaty.

He came in to find his dad opening a can of food for the kitten.

"Did you go running? That's new," he said. "But don't forget to take care of your familiar before you go out. It's your responsibility."

"Oh, yeah. Sorry," he said automatically. "I just, you know, felt like going out."

"It's nice to see you taking an interest in physical fitness. I could help you draw up a plan, if you're interested."

"Thanks, Dad. But I think I'm okay. I'm going to go get in the shower."

"Before you go, did you think of a name for your kitten?"

"Oh, I was thinking of naming her ..." And suddenly his mouth said the word, "Tseluna."

"Seluna?"

"No," he said, knowing that was wrong. "It's Tseluna, with a T."

"Why did you name her that?"

"Uh … It just seemed right?"

He went into the bathroom to take a shower. Standing in the hot spray, he wondered again, and not for the last time, just what he had gotten himself into. He was utterly conflicted. He simply did not know how to feel. His head was a constantly shifting mix of confusion, puzzlement, terror, and excitement.

When he returned to his bedroom to change, she was still sitting on the bed in human form.

"You can read my mind, can't you?" he asked. She nodded.

"Yes. I can not only hear what you're thinking, I can also remember all your memories. It made for an interesting night last night."

"So … You know everything about me. Everything. Even that I … I called them 'nummies'," he said, covering his face. "Do you have any idea how embarrassing that is? I literally don't know anything about you."

"*Baka*! You're my familiar!" she said. "Of course, I should know everything about you."

"How many familiars have you had?" he asked.

"You need to get ready for the academy," she said, ignoring his question. "It wouldn't do to be late to show them your new familiar."

3

A FAMILIAR CLASS

(99 TRALONGS)

RORY ARRIVED AT SCHOOL carrying Tseluna in kitten form. He approached his gaming friends, Gabe, Larry, and Fred, who were in another class.

"Well met, Milords," he said, following the Protocol.

"Well met, Lord RazorFell," they said in turn, using the name of his character in the game they played on Wednesday evenings. He inclined his head and continued on through the crowded hallways.

He arrived at his home room and took his seat. Once he was seated, Tseluna climbed up and perched on his shoulder.

"Hey! I thought you said cats were 'incredibly trite' as familiars," Buck said. He had a striped tabby as a familiar and had been one of those most offended by Rory's intemperate remarks the previous day.

"I ... I guess I spoke too soon," Rory said, trying politely to smooth things over.

"Hey! No worries. Welcome to Team Cat!"

Aimee walked over and planted herself in front of him.

"I thought you wanted a strong familiar you could battle with," she said.

"Appearances can be deceiving," he said. Aimee stared at Tseluna. Then she shook her head and walked to her seat, as the teacher, Mr. Burton, came in with his owl familiar, and called the class to order.

"Put your books away and get out your pencils," he said. "Don't forget the test this morning."

With horror, Rory realized he'd completely forgotten to study for the test. He was certain to fail because it was over a piece of ancient literature he hadn't bothered to read.

He received the test paper and read the first question, "Where is the 'Song of Magnolia' set?" He drew a blank and started to go to the next question when he heard "Borelia" in his head. He wrote it into the blank. "Who lifts the enchantment on the princess?" He waited a moment and Tseluna passed him the answer to that one as well: "Roland." He answered the rest of the questions in this fashion.

As the papers were collected, there was chatter in the room as the students relaxed after the test.

"Rory Soletsa?" Mr. Burton called.

"Sir?"

"I see you've got a new familiar," he said. "Would you come to the front of the room and introduce your familiar to us?"

Rory walked slowly to the front of the room, feeling the stares of everyone on his back. He turned and looked out over the faces in the classroom. Buck gave him a huge smile and a thumbs up. Aimee had a guarded expression.

"I know I said yesterday, I wasn't going to have a cat for a familiar," he began. "And I might have said some other dumb things. But last night some kids wanted to kill this kitten because they said black cats were evil. And, well, I fell in love with her. Her name is Tseluna."

"Thank you, Mr. Soletsa," the teacher said as there was a

quiet round of applause while Rory took his seat again. "Now, turn to page 234 of your textbook for the next lesson."

After two hours, it was finally lunchtime. Rory stood and stretched. Normally, he might have brought a lunch, but he'd been otherwise occupied this morning, so he went to the cafeteria. He waited forever in line until he could grab a roast beef sandwich and a bag of chips. Once he'd paid, he slipped out of the cafeteria and walked to "his" bench.

Behind the flower garden, there was a bench you couldn't see from the sidewalk. You'd never know it was there if you didn't already know. Nobody ever sat there and Rory had come to think of it as his. He found dealing with other people tedious and was happy to have a quiet place to escape to for a few minutes at lunch time.

"It's meat. Would you like some?" he asked, as he unwrapped the sandwich, tore off a bit of meat, and offered it to Tseluna. She accepted one bite after another that he offered to her. Once she was satisfied, he wolfed the rest of the sandwich down himself.

"Why do you hide back here?" Aimee said, coming up from the path.

"It's restful," Rory said. "Dealing with other people is tiresome."

"Is there any more to your story about getting a familiar?" Aimee asked.

"What else would there be?" Rory said. She scowled at him.

"There's just something odd," she said. "I've been studying how to visualize magical flows. And your familiar bond looks weird."

"Weird?" he said, breaking out in a sweat. "What do you mean?"

"Well, normally, in a familiar bond, the magical energy flows from the owner to the familiar. But yours flows backward." She peered at him again and shook her head.

"Huh," he said, sweating and trying to sound puzzled and non-committal.

"It's almost like you're the familiar and …" she started to say, but then the bell rang and Rory got up.

"We'd better get back," he said, very glad to have cut short that conversation.

Back in the classroom, Mr. Burton handed their test papers back.

"Only one student got full marks," he announced to the class. "Rory Soletsa."

"You only missed one," he said, handing the paper back to Aimee. She glared at Rory, who looked away pretending he didn't see the unbridled fury in her eyes. She prided herself on being at the top of the class and took anyone outscoring her personally. Especially, he thought, when she knew full well they couldn't have scored that high without cheating somehow. He readied himself to deal with her anger soon enough.

"This afternoon," Mr. Burton said, with his owl on his shoulder. "We're going to begin learning about using offensive and defensive magic. Today, we're going to learn to cast fireballs!"

Rory heard that and quit listening, since he'd taught himself how to cast fireballs a year ago and didn't need to hear someone describe how to do it.

After forty minutes of lecture about theory, Mr. Burton took them out to the range. He asked them to form a line and then each student was invited to cast a fireball down the range. Rory ended up near the end of the line.

He watched while most of the students produced grape- or tangelo-sized fireballs. Most fizzled out before reaching the target. When it was his turn, he asked, "The biggest I can make?"

Mr. Burton nodded.

He heard Tseluna's voice in his head, "Don't. Just make a small one, like grapefruit-sized."

He closed his eyes, and tried to catch just a small amount of the overflowing magical power that was at his disposal. He spoke the word of power and a canteloupe-sized fireball flew true toward the target and blasted it into fragments. Everyone else in the class gasped and then whooped with excitement.

"Excellent, Mr. Soletsa," Mr. Burton said. "Very well done indeed! That showed good control!"

"Suck up," Aimee hissed at him, still stinging from the test.

When the last student cast their fireball, they were nearly at the end of the school day, so Mr. Burton dismissed the class from there and everyone ran back to grab their bags and head home. But Rory was in a bad mood. He went stomping off into the woods behind the school. Having Aimee sneer at him had made him angry and he wanted to blow off steam. He felt like he needed to hit something or break something.

"You need to calm yourself down," Tseluna said reasonably in his head.

"No. I need to smash something. Or burn something!" he replied. He started to prepare a fireball when suddenly his magic dropped to zero. The sudden feeling of powerlessness made him panic.

"No," Tseluna said, bluntly. "You're far too powerful now to let yourself give in to these kinds of childish impulses. Let me show you what I mean."

Suddenly, he felt a twist in his gut and he was standing in the middle of a grassy meadow on a mountain top. His ears popped. He worked his jaw to equalize the pressure, then shivered. It was chilly with a strong breeze. Tseluna was standing beside him in human form.

"Wait! Did you just teleport us? Without the Blink Network?" Rory asked, stunned. "I didn't think that was possible!"

"Hang on. Remember in class when he asked you to make the strongest fireball you could and I told you to make a smaller one? Let's try that again. Go ahead now and make the largest fireball you can but direct it straight up, where it won't hurt anything."

Rory checked and found his magic had returned. He prepared a fireball, but this time, he poured everything he could into making it bigger and bigger and bigger. And when he finally couldn't add any more, he spoke the word of power.

A crushing wave of heat bore down on him as a giant fireball went up into the sky. It was hundreds of feet across and left a scorched circle dozens of feet across on the grass. He felt his hair and eyebrows singe. The shoulders of his shirt started smoldering. The fireball ascended into the heavens like a second sun.

Rory stood there with his mouth hanging open.

"Do you understand now, what a moment's inattention or loss of control can do when you're playing with forces like these? Think how many people you could have killed without even trying!"

Rory looked down, humbled both by her sharp words and his realization of what might have happened without Tseluna reining him in.

"I'm sorry. I will remember," he said, staring at his feet. "Thank you."

She tousled his hair and then hugged him.

"It gets easier after a few hundred years," she said.

4

A FAMILIAR TASTE
(98 TRALONGS)

O N SATURDAY MORNING, Rory tried to resist getting up for his morning run.

"Do I really have to go this morning?" he asked. "It's Saturday! Can't I just take a rest today?"

Tseluna held up a finger and said, "If you don't learn to obey promptly, I will be compelled to punish you."

Grumbling, he dragged himself out of bed.

"You're Tseloony," he thought to himself.

"I heard that," she said in his head. He cringed to be reminded, once again, that she was constantly in his head reading his mind.

He put his shoes on and headed out on his usual route. Tseluna appeared behind him in a human guise, wearing clothes, and matched his pace.

When he got to the graveyard and went to turn off, she directed him to continue straight and kept running him twice as far out before making the turn. She directed him to take a trail that led through a forest with hills, logs to jump over, and places with sand and loose soil. In the middle, there was a long, metal bridge that led over a small valley with a slow, muddy stream at the bottom. Eventually, it hooked up with another road. Finally, Tseluna directed him to turn toward home. Gratefully, he headed back, now starting to get really tired.

"Pick up the pace," Tseluna subvocalized to him. Rory sped up a little.

"More," she said. He increased his stride a bit. He was now starting to get short of breath. He tried to back off, when he felt her poke his back with her finger and there was a sudden jolt of pain that shot through his whole body.

"Yow!" he yelped and put on a burst of speed. He was now seriously out of breath and began to pant and gasp.

"Just a little more," she said. "Go! Go!"

He was nearly at the point of passing out when he turned the last corner and found he was alone. He stopped and panted until he could breathe again and then slowly walked for the last little bit until he was home. He returned to his room, to find her smiling cheerfully at him from his bed.

Once he had showered and broken his fast, Tseluna teleported them to what appeared to be an old orchard with apple trees laden with fruit.

"Where are we?" Rory asked. "How are there apples at this time of year? You can't travel through time, can you?"

"No," Tseluna said. "It's not possible to travel through time. Not even a demon can do that. No, we've just traveled to the southern hemisphere. It's fall here and the apples are ripe. Before we head back, we should pick some and take them with us."

"How will we pick them without a ladder?" he asked.

"Ah!" she said, pleased. "That's exactly what I want you to learn: how to exert forces on objects with magic and how to pick things up, which is considerably more difficult."

She spread a beach towel out on the ground and sat down.

"Come here," she said. She had him lie down with his head in her lap and she gently stroked his hair and twirled it around her fingers while she explained the theory.

"Got it?" she said finally.

"I think so," he said. "Let me try."

"Try pushing first," she said.

He tried to gather just a little bit of power and focused on an apple. When he spoke a word of power, the apple splattered into pulp like he'd hit it with a bat. He recoiled.

"Aren't you glad we didn't try to pull it toward us?" she said patiently. "Try again."

He tried again and eventually, with practice, he was able to calibrate the force until he could bat them or just give them a tap and have them swing back and forth.

"Good. Now try to pull them to you," she said, with her hands on his shoulders.

He pulled one down, it flew to him, and he caught it.

"This is awesome," he said. And he took a bite. "These are good apples too!"

"Next, try to lift one up and make it float."

After licking the juice from his fingers, he tried to lift one up. This indeed proved to be much more difficult. He could push the apple up, but when he tried to make it float, it would roll off one way or the other and fall. He tried over and over until he was thoroughly frustrated.

"Hmm," she said. "I think I know another way we might practice this skill. But I think that's enough for the morning. Let's just pick some and take them home."

Rory collected a dozen of the best looking apples and carried them home wrapped up in the towel.

After training, Rory had worked up a good appetite and had lunch with his dad while Tseluna lounged nearby in kitten form.

"Do you want to go to the summer festival this afternoon?" Rory's dad asked, munching on an apple after lunch. "I can give you some money."

"Eh. Not really," Rory said, carrying Tseluna back to his bedroom. "It's mostly kid's stuff."

"I'll bet you'd feel different if you had a girlfriend."

"Dad!" Rory huffed, rolling his eyes.

"What is this summer festival?" Tseluna asked in his head.

"Oh. There are games and activities for kids, food, and, after dark, they have a pyrotechnics show."

"Well, aren't you going to take me?"

"Do you really want to go?"

"Sure."

"Hey, Dad?" Rory called. "On second thought, I'll take you up on that."

Rory left with Tseluna in kitten form and a 1000 spess bill he had extracted from his dad. Once they turned the corner, she leapt into the bushes and then emerged as a young black woman, seemingly about Rory's age, wearing an unfamiliar school uniform.

"Whoa!" Rory said. "Can you transform into anything?"

"Only things that I've studied very, very carefully. You need to get every detail right or it doesn't work. But I know people inside and out, so they're no problem."

"It's unbelievable," Rory said.

"Now, let's go to the festival," she said, taking his arm.

The festival was set up around the pavilion in the park where Rory had first met Tseluna. Since it was still a little early, it was packed with kids playing the games. They took one walk all the way around to look at everything, then a second time around where Rory paid for Tseluna to play a few of the kiddie games.

At the ring toss, they each bought three rings. Rory tossed his and all three bounced off and missed. Tseluna tossed her three rings and hit the three highest scoring bottles. The carny, obviously disgusted, let her pick whichever stuffed toy she wanted. She picked a large, white bear, then held it up next to Rory.

"I picked this one because it reminds me of you," she said, with a chuckle. Rory wanted to crawl under a rock with embarrassment and Tseluna laughed at his discomfort. After teasing Rory for a few minutes, she handed the bear to a little girl who had been eying it, and who squealed with delight to receive it.

Afterward, she took his arm again and made him lead her over to the food. He bought her some skewers of roasted chicken and then took her to the bench by the stream where he had given her milk the first time he'd met her.

"Would you like anything to drink?" he asked, handing her the skewers.

"A bottle of milk would be nice," she said, licking her lips.

He walked over to the concession stand and stood in line until it was his turn and purchased two bottles of milk. When he went to go back, he turned and found himself face-to-face with Aimee.

"Oh! What a surprise to see you here," he said.

Aimee grabbed his hand and dragged him back behind the line of stalls selling concessions at the festival. Then she turned and faced him.

"What's happening to you?" she asked. "I know we're not close like when we were little. But something is going on."

"What do you mean?" Rory asked, only too aware that his responses were being carefully monitored.

"Who is that girl you're with?"

"Huh? Oh. That's …" he started to say and then found himself unable to continue when Tseluna stopped him.

"It's not a hard question, Rory! She's been clinging to you!"

"Uh …"

"Why are you being so evasive? Why can't you just talk to me?"

"I … can't explain," he said, finally. "I'm sorry."

"Oh! Rory Soletsa, you make me so angry!" she said. She threw her hands up and walked away in a huff.

After Aimee left, he fell into a profound reverie. Tseluna came up behind him, took one of the bottles of milk he was still absently holding, and then put her arm around him.

"You're right, Sugar," she said. "She does. If you weren't so dense, you'd have noticed before."

"Stop reading my mind!" he said. She tousled his hair, which only made him angrier.

"You're so cute when you're angry."

Rory squired Tseluna around the festival again and bought her some cotton candy which she tasted and rejected, so he ate it. When he took his first bite, he realized he hadn't had any cotton candy since the last time he came to the festival with his mom. The memory made him extremely nostalgic—even a little weepy. Tseluna turned to him, pursed her lips, and reached a finger to the corner of his eye and collected a tear, then popped it into her mouth.

"It's okay, Sugar," she said, gently patting his face. "I'm here." But Rory was not comforted.

It was getting dark and all of the elemental lights came on. They were preparing the magical pyrotechnic display when Tseluna suddenly dug her fingernails into his arm.

"There's another demon nearby," she said. "We should get away from people."

Rory led her to the nearest bridge where they walked across the field and entered the forest just as the pyrotechnics display began. Once they were out of sight of the festival, Tseluna gestured at the path, but then pulled Rory out of sight behind a big tree.

"I think this is the demon that sent the direwolves after us," she said. "I've left an illusion of us on the path."

"I can't see anything," Rory said.

"It's an illusion of our magical energies. Demons are creatures of magic and we are more likely to pay attention to magical energies than physical appearance. Demons will only materialize if they want to take some action that impacts the physical plane."

They watched and waited while the pyrotechnics display went on overhead.

Rory saw the other demon materialize in the path near where Tseluna had gestured. They did not seem to have a carefully constructed human body, like Tseluna. They were more rough and unfinished looking. The geometry of their limbs and joints was subtly wrong. They appeared to be looking around for them.

"Stay under cover," Tseluna warned.

Rory stayed behind Tseluna and the massive tree trunk. Then he heard, "Rory?"

Aimee appeared on the path from the playground.

Rory saw the demon begin to gesture at Aimee.

"No!" he shouted and, raising his shield, he charged blindly into the path toward Aimee. A powerful blow hit him from behind and knocked him into her and they both fell. His shield blunted the strange demon's attack, but left his clothes smoldering and gave him first-degree burns over his shoulder and back.

He screamed with pain and in anticipation of the next attack, but it didn't come. When he looked up, Tseluna had assumed her normal appearance and was standing between them and the other demon.

"Who ... What is that?" Aimee whispered.

The demons spoke with one another in a horrifying language of shrieks, clicks, and trills and then lit up the sky with a bewildering array of bright colors and flashes. After a moment, the other demon was gone. Tseluna turned toward Rory.

"Rory!" she said, in a menacing tone. "Come here."

Rory stood and approached Tseluna.

"You disobeyed me," she said. "My direct order."

"But," he stammered. "But I ... I couldn't ..."

"I've told you that punishment is counter-productive, but sometimes it's necessary to send a message," she said. "Do I need to punish you?"

Rory swallowed and lifted his chin.

"I will accept your punishment," he said, putting on a brave face.

"What if your punishment is to kill her?" Tseluna said, indicating Aimee.

Rory felt like he'd taken a punch to the gut. He became completely unstrung, his eyes filled with tears, and he fell to his knees sobbing. He knew she could take control of his body and make him do anything.

"No, Tseluna!" he pleaded. "No! Please! Not that!"

"Who or what are you?" Aimee said, coming forward. "What are you doing to him?"

"I am Tseluna," Tseluna said.

"Wait!" Aimee said. "You're his familiar?"

"No," Tseluna clarified. "He is my familiar."

"What?" she said, then remembered her observation of his familiar bond. "But ... No! You can't do that!"

"He is mine," Tseluna said, turning her bright, yellow eyes on Aimee.

"What are you?" she asked.

"I am a demon," she replied. "I was not planning on having my presence here revealed. It would be ... inconvenient if people tried to interfere with our work."

"I'm sorry, Tseluna!" Rory bawled, tears streaming down his face and dripping off his nose. On his knees, he held onto her legs and put his head on her feet. "I'm sorry. I'm sorry! I just wanted her to be safe. She's my dearest friend. Please don't make me hurt my friend."

"Get up and stop this display," Tseluna said.

Rory struggled to his feet, wiped his eyes, and tried to master himself.

"Now, will you be disobedient again?" she asked.

"No, Tseluna," he said, looking down. "I won't ... I will be obedient. I promise."

"And you," Tseluna said, looking at Aimee. "You have no idea what I am capable of. Please do not mention my presence to anyone until our work is complete."

"When will that be, exactly?" Aimee asked, her eyes narrowing.

"Once your school resumes, you may tell anyone anything you like," Tseluna replied. "May I have your word on the matter?"

"I swear," Aimee said. "I will tell no-one."

Tseluna nodded and, in a voice heavy with emphasis, said, "I will know if you do." Then to Rory, "Come. You still have much training to accomplish."

"Yes, Tseluna," he said, chastened, and turned to follow her.

"Rory!" Aimee called. Rory turned and looked back. "Thank you for saving me."

Rory, still sniffling, gave her a wan smile, waved, then turned and followed Tseluna into the forest, toward home.

5

AN UNFAMILIAR PLACE
(97 TRALONGS)

T HE NEXT MORNING, Rory awoke with an erection. Eyes still closed, he indulged himself with an erotic fantasy.

"That's quite an imagination you have," Tseluna purred in his ear.

"Don't read my mind, if it bothers you," he said, shifting his fantasy so it included her.

"Oh, now you're just trying to provoke me," she said. "Be careful what you wish for."

Rory felt his face turn red.

"Maybe I'll just take a cold shower this morning," he said, starting to get up. Tseluna pushed him back into the bed.

"Here. Let me take care of this."

She offered him a breast and then reached down and grasped his painful erection.

She let him nurse while she gently stroked his penis. She teased him until both breasts were emptied. Then, with clinical detachment, she quickly brought him to climax and wiped her hand off on his stomach.

"What am I to you?" Rory asked, anguished.

Tseluna regarded him with a thoughtful expression. "Hmm. Like a racehorse, maybe? I'm making a huge investment and taking a big risk with you."

"But ... You kiss me and toy with my emotions. Why? What does it mean?"

"Perhaps it's what I think will be most effective in helping you achieve your full potential."

He covered his face and whispered, "But why are you ... n-nursing me? I mean, I can't say I don't love it, but ..."

"Ah. You haven't noticed yet. Come here," she said, pulling him to his feet and guiding him over to a mirror. He looked at himself and then turned and looked again.

"Am I taller? Were my muscles always this clearly defined?"

"I'm speeding up your growth, a bit. And multiplying the effects of your training. Plus, I think it helps you bond with me."

"But what does it mean? To you?"

"You're thinking about it too hard. Just relax. Enjoy the ride," she said, patting his face. "Now get dressed. We need to go."

Rory excused himself, cleaned up with a washcloth, then returned to put on his running clothes. He headed out on his morning run with Tseluna.

After he returned, he showered and returned to his room to get dressed.

"You say you are a demon," Rory said, pulling his pants on. "What exactly is a demon?"

"I come from a different dimension where magic is far more plentiful and magical knowledge is far more advanced."

"Dimension?" Rory asked.

"Oh. I guess we haven't talked about that. There are thousands of ... well, some would say, an infinite number of dimensions. The whole universe you experience is but one such dimension. Almost all the dimensions are non-viable—lifeless. All it takes is one little thing to go wrong and life gets snuffed out or never develops.

"Some dimensions have huge amounts of available magic. Some have basically none. This dimension is on the low end. That's why the magic here is so weak. That's also why you don't generally see demons come here—it's uncomfortable for them. Like it would be uncomfortable for you to go someplace where the air is very thin."

"Where does your magic come from then?"

"I can store magic. So, I can even go to a dimension that has no magic and use my stored magic—for a time."

"How long can you stay before you start to run out?"

"In this dimension? Oh, much longer than your lifetime. Even in a zero-magic dimension, I could stay for many, many years. But, if I stayed too long, I might end up stuck there, unable to use magic even to get out. Speaking of which ..." Tseluna gestured and a circular region appeared in front of them that showed a landscape at once familiar and unfamiliar. He could see the back of a human-scale dwelling, but the building style was unusual. Tseluna took his hand.

"Come on, Sugar! Don't be shy!"

They stepped through the portal which closed behind them, and Rory found himself in a beautiful garden. They had emerged on a grassy sward that bordered a small pond. There were low hedges, cunningly trimmed to look like mountains in the distance. A beautiful tree was in blossom. She led him under the tree and invited him to look up.

The branches were laden with flowers. The blossoms were pink with five petals. Bees were active so much that the whole tree simply buzzed.

"Ah! You're lucky! These are sakura blossoms," she said. "They only bloom for a short time. People here revere them as a symbol of the ephemeral nature of life."

Suddenly the door of the house slid open and a wizened, elderly man came out.

"*Tadaima*, Hideyoshi-san," Tseluna said, inclining her head. Rory did a double-take when he looked at Tseluna and perceived she was now wearing a light colored robe with a bold, brilliant pattern of chrysanthemum blossoms tied with a broad, pink strip of fabric.

"*Okaeri*, Tseluna-sama!" the old man said, bowing very low indeed.

"This is Hideyoshi-san," she said to Rory in his language. "We are in a place called Japan. This place has basically no magic natively."

"But ..." Rory said, after checking. "I can still use magic."

"Since you're my familiar," Tseluna said. "You can get magic through your bond with me."

Hideyoshi-san began to speak and Tseluna spoke with him for a minute, then turned to Rory.

"Hideyoshi-san would like to speak with you, so I will translate. He asks first if you are in love with me."

"Yes, I am," Rory replied instantly, blushing.

"*Hai*," Tseluna translated, as if the answer weren't already apparent. Hideyoshi-san grinned, showing mostly toothless gums. He spoke for a long time and Tseluna translated for him.

"I met her when I was a young man. She saved my life, and we went on many adventures together. But now I am an old man, and I am content with my garden and my memories."

Suddenly, he said something to Tseluna and then bustled off back into his house.

"He said we should sit over there, under the pergola and he will bring us tea."

As they walked toward the pergola, Rory noticed large golden fish swimming lazily in the pond. He could see other white and red fish farther out.

"This is a beautiful garden," he said. "I've never seen a more peaceful place."

"It will please Hideyoshi-san when I tell him you said so," Tseluna smiled.

In a few moments, the old man returned with a tray with three small cups and a teapot. He poured tea for each of them.

"*Dozo!*" he said, setting the cup before Rory. Rory watched Tseluna for hints regarding what to do.

"*Itadakimasu!*" she said, then picked up the cup and took a tiny sip.

"*Umai!*" she pronounced. She looked at Rory.

"*Itadakimasu!*" he said, as best he could. She nodded. He tasted his. It was warm and had a light, pleasant, aromatic flavor, unlike anything he'd had before.

"It's good," he said. Tseluna translated and the old man grinned.

"I brought you here because I want Hideyoshi-san to demonstrate something for you," Tseluna said. Then she spoke several sentences in Japanese to Hideyoshi-san who grinned again and stood up.

"There is a martial art I want to teach you," she said. "But it's more than a martial art. It's a way of thinking and approaching problems. I could show you myself, but I think it will be more effective if Hideyoshi-san demonstrates. It's called 'aikido'," she said. She closed her eyes for a moment.

"Don't panic, but I've cut off your access to my magic for a moment—just to make sure you don't use it by mistake. Go ahead and try to hit or catch or wrestle or push him."

"The old man? Won't he get hurt?"

"Just try," she said.

Rory stood and, feeling silly, walked over and tried to reach out to grab the old man. Suddenly, he was lying on his back looking up at the sky. The old man grinned cheerfully down at him. He got to his feet and tried again, faster. This time, he landed even harder and had the wind knocked out of him. It took him a minute to get his breath back.

Rory stood again and tried a different approach. This time, he balanced and tried punching. No sooner had he thrown a punch, but the old man had stepped inside the reach of his arm, pivoted, and used his own momentum to throw him off-balance.

Rory tried one more time. He stood and then suddenly charged, trying to grab the old man. But, like quicksilver, he slipped to the side and pushed down on Rory's head when he was over-extended and his face plowed into the grass. He came up spitting grass and bugs.

"Okay, okay," he said, putting his hands up, palms out. "I'm convinced."

The old man laughed and bowed to him. Rory centered himself and bowed to the old man, trying to bow even more deeply. Hideyoshi-san looked pleased and spoke a quick flood of words to Tseluna.

"You are a quick study," Tseluna translated. "You learn fast and are thoughtful and polite. He approves of you. We should go back now."

"Already?"

"Time runs at different rates in different dimensions. We have only been here about two hours, yet in your dimension, nearly six hours have passed. We need to use the time we have wisely."

"You mean, because you're only allowed to train me for a certain amount of time?"

"Well, that doesn't matter so much. The clock started when I formed the familiar bond with you. Even if we went to a slow dimension, time for us would still run at the same rate for us and would count the same. No, I was just thinking you should get home in time for dinner with your father."

"Oh, right."

Tseluna stood and then inclined her head to Hideyoshi-san, who again bowed very deeply indeed. Then she opened the portal and, taking Rory's hand, led him back through it into his bedroom.

He looked at the clock and saw it was indeed nearly dinner time. He ran out to the kitchen and decided to fix a stir fry. He cut up meat and began to fry it while he cut up vegetables. In a few minutes his dad came home and set the table.

Once the stir-fry was finished Rory carried the pan to the table and set it on a pad. They both served themselves.

"*Itadakimasu!*" Rory said. His dad looked at him curiously.

"What did you say?"

"It's just something that people say when they're about to eat or drink something," he said.

"Oh."

6

A FAMILIAR STORY

(94 TRALONGS)

THE LAST DAY OF SCHOOL was a half-day. Rory arrived on time with Tseluna in kitten form. There were no serious academic activities, but the class played a few games and Mr. Burton spent some time inviting each student to mention what they were doing for the summer. When it was Rory's turn, he stood to speak, but then Tseluna took control of his mouth.

"I applied for a scholarship to learn battle magic," he said. "And I won a full ride. So, I'm going to be training the whole time to get ready for a tournament at the end of the summer. I look forward to telling you all about it next year!"

Everyone cheered, except for Aimee, who looked at him—and through him—and he wondered if she could tell that it wasn't really him speaking. He didn't suppose that he would be able to tell, so flawless was Tseluna's impersonation of him. He returned to his seat and looked again at the clock, anticipating the end of class.

Finally, the bell rang, and the students charged out of the school, ecstatic for the summer to finally begin.

"Today," Tseluna said, as they strolled back toward home. "I want you to learn how to cast a sleep spell."

"Is that really battle magic, though?" Rory asked, with kind of a sneer.

"You might be surprised," she said. "Sometimes it's exactly what you want. But I really want you to learn it because it requires a certain kind of finesse and light touch that—speaking honestly—you currently lack."

Rory scowled.

"Don't be like that, Sugar," she laughed. "It's easy, fun, and good practice."

They turned off into the park and went into the forest.

"Let's start with squirrels," Tseluna said. "They're perfect to practice on. What you need to do is very gently stroke the hypothalamus like this."

Rory watched as she gestured at a squirrel high up in a tree. It went limp and tumbled out of the tree, then awoke in a panic as it bounced off the ground. It was funny in a mean-spirited way to see the squirrel's consternation.

"Now you give it a try, Sugar!"

Rory collected some power, spotted another squirrel, gestured, and spoke a word of power. The squirrel's head exploded with a pop and it fell to the ground, limp and lifeless.

Rory cringed, devastated to have killed the little thing.

"See? This here is exactly what I'm talking about," Tseluna said. "Finesse! Just be glad we're not practicing on babies at the daycare."

Rory couldn't help himself and started laughing.

"Okay!" Tseluna said. "Now try again. GENTLY."

Rory spotted another squirrel and, dialing back the power as much as he could, he tried very, very gently to touch its hypothalamus. No effect. So he added in just a bit more power and tried again. No effect. Frustrated, he added a bit more and tried again. Still nothing. Then he got angry and tried again. Pop! He looked down as he was splattered with a mist of squirrel blood and tissue.

"Ew," Tseluna said. "Here. Let me try."

Suddenly, Rory felt Tseluna take control of his body. She marshaled a small amount of energy and then with a very light touch, she reached out and just gave the tiniest stroke to a squirrel and it conked out, sprawling out on the branch, like she'd pushed a switch.

"Now you try again," she said.

Rory flexed his fingers, back under his control, and spotted another squirrel. With a better sense for what to do, he tried again and got it on the first try.

"I did it! I did it!" he cheered. Tseluna patted his head.

"Good boy!" she said, and he felt the now familiar little bump of pleasure as she rewarded him. "Just so you know, I'm doing pretty much the same thing with your pleasure center. And, be aware that if you are disobedient, I can do the same with any number of pain centers in your brain too.

"Now, at some point, you should try practicing on people. We could walk around at night looking for someone who can't get to sleep and give them a little help. But, first, you might look for a bad guy to practice on—just in case."

When they got home, Rory fixed a sandwich for himself.

"Do you want anything?" he asked Tseluna.

"No, thanks."

"Would you like some coffee?"

"No, thank you," Tseluna said. "I don't like hot things."

"But we had that ... What was that with Hideyoshi-san?"

"That was tea," she said. "But he knows my taste, so it was only warm and not hot."

"Would you like some milk?"

"Sure," she said with a smile.

After lunch, Tseluna teleported them to a remote, U-shaped, rocky valley with a wide-open area near a little clear lake.

"Today," Tseluna said. "I'm going to begin your training in aikido."

"Could you put on clothes?" Rory said, squeezing his eyes closed. "Otherwise it's too … distracting."

She rolled her yellow eyes, but then was wearing a kind of open white jacket and dark pleated trousers tied with a broad belt.

"Ooh. Do I get a uniform too?"

"If you study and practice diligently," Tseluna said. "First, answer me this: what did you discover when you tried to touch Hideyoshi-san?"

"He was using my own force and momentum against me," Rory said, promptly. Tseluna inclined her head in acknowledgment.

"Yes," she said. "Precisely. You don't try to contend with your opponent's strength directly, but to avoid and redirect it to use against them.

"And this principle is not just about physical attacks. As a boy, you have been trained to have an unfortunate tendency to want to compete with your opponents directly, to see 'who is stronger' or 'whose dick is bigger'."

Rory blushed and looked down.

"Let's begin with meditation," Tseluna said, smoothly moving into *seiza* position. "You need to cultivate an attitude of calm readiness."

Rory tried to assume the *seiza* position the same way, but overbalanced and fell over. He got up onto his knees.

"Now, close your eyes and focus on your breathing. In … And out. Count your breaths. Relax. But now open your eyes and take note of your surroundings. But don't lose count!"

After several hours of training, Tseluna teleported them to just outside Rory's front door. Tseluna had transformed her human form. Now, she was wearing a stylish, conservative suit and her eyes looked like dark, human eyes, rather than her usual bright yellow cat eyes.

"Today, I'm planning to introduce myself to your father. Leave the talking to me," Tseluna said. "Literally."

Rory shrugged, baffled. But then they walked into the living room, where suddenly he heard himself addressing his father.

"Hi, Dad," he found himself saying. "I wanted to introduce you to Mrs. T. I saw a scholarship at school that looked cool, so I applied for it and I got it! Mrs. T can tell you more about how it works."

"That's great!" Rory's dad said. "I'm pleased to see you looking for and taking advantage of opportunities like these!"

"Yes, Mr. Soletsa," Tseluna smoothly took over. "This is a scholarship program for students interested in learning about using magic for defense. Rory placed near the top in the applicant pool, so he's been awarded a full scholarship. It will mean intensive training for him all summer followed by attendance at a special tournament overseas. All expenses paid!"

"It's nice to meet you, Mrs. T," Rory's dad said. "If there's anything I can do to support Rory, I'm happy to provide it. Thank you so much for taking him on."

"It's nice to meet you too," Tseluna said with a disarming smile. "I'll be personally training and coaching Rory all summer, so you'll probably see me around. He will be very busy, but it shouldn't impact you at all."

"Would you care to stay for dinner?" Rory's dad asked Tseluna.

"Why, thank you for the invitation," she said. "That would be very nice!"

Rory started to roll his eyes, when he heard Tseluna's sharp voice in his head, "If you give even the tiniest sign that suggests we are not being absolutely honest and aboveboard, I will punish you severely and without fail."

Rory froze and kept his expression studiedly neutral.

After a pleasant dinner with his dad, Rory did his summer homework with tutoring by Tseluna who, as it turned out, seemingly knew everything there was to know about anything.

"Look," Tseluna said. "It's not hard. As one thing increases, what could the other thing do?"

"It could go up?"

"Right! Or what else?"

"It could go down?"

"Or ..."

"What?"

"Well, it could stay the same—or approach some limit. Plus, there's one other possibility."

"What's that?"

"Chaos. Impossible to predict. Like me," she grinned.

"What about me?" Rory asked.

"Oh, Sugar! You're so sweet," Tseluna said, patting his face. "But so predictable."

At 9pm, Rory was getting ready for bed at Tseluna's insistence. Angling to stay up a little longer, Rory decided to try to get her talking.

"So, are you ever going to tell me what this is all about?" he asked.

"I don't think you're going to like the answer."

"I think I've got a pretty good idea already, so why don't you try me?"

She heaved a big sigh and looked at him with her brilliant, yellow eyes.

"Every 500 tralongs—you can think of it like a year, though it's a little longer—there's a ... tournament where trainers pit their familiars against one another. The winning trainer ... Well, let's just say there's a certain amount of prestige involved."

"What does the familiar get?"

She looked at him.

"Oh," he said.

"If ... No! When! When you win, I will free you from your familiar bond."

"What if I don't win?"

"The battles in the tournament are to the death."

He felt a sense of rising panic.

"So, if I die, that's one thing. But ... if I win, you'll just dump me?"

"*Baka*! What are you asking? Why would you want to stay as a familiar? Don't you understand?" she said. "I captured you and bound you to my will! I'm a monster!"

"No! No, you're not! You're not a monster!" Rory said. And he knelt at her feet and raised his arms, supplicating, while he looked up at her. "You're a goddess. You're my goddess. And I worship you!"

"*Baka*," she said, more quietly, rolling her eyes.

"Really!" he insisted. "More than anything, I wanted to learn how to use battle magic and to have a partner that I could stand together with. And you've given me that! I love you! I want to stay with you forever! For as long as I have!"

"Get up," she said. "You're embarrassing yourself."

His face red, he got up and sat on the edge of the bed. Then he tried to draw out the conversation a little longer.

"This tournament sounds pretty sketchy—like a dogfight or a cockfight. Is that really allowed?"

"Well, it's not exactly legal," she admitted. "But it's been going on for tens of thousands of tralongs and the D-Force hasn't shut it down yet. In any event, I'm the one accepting the risk of that."

"The D-Force?"

"Oh. It's sort of like a demon police force. They mostly enforce demon rules about trans-dimensional interference."

"Trans-dimensional interference ... You mean like what you're doing to me?"

Tseluna grinned and winked at him.

"So ... What are the rules of this tournament?"

"Contestants have to catch a familiar and train it for no more than 100 tralongs—that's about three months. The familiars have to pass a series of qualifying rounds and then are ranked for the tournament."

"You seem pretty familiar with all this. How many times have you done it?"

"I haven't counted. Maybe a hundred times?"

"How many times have you won?"

She looked away.

"Not even once?"

"Not yet. But I think you've got a good chance. Well, pretty good anyway."

His blood chilled as he considered his odds.

"What makes you think I've got a good chance?"

"A few things. Partly, I know what I'm doing better. And partly, you seem to want to learn. I think that will make a big difference."

"What happened last year?"

She looked off into the distance.

"This is the second time I'm trying a human. I picked one last time too. That time, I picked an adult—he was in his 40s. I thought picking someone who was already an expert in magical attacks would be an advantage. But, instead, he could never accept the bond. He fought it to the end. That's partly why I picked someone younger this time."

She pointed at the bed.

"Now quit stalling and go to sleep. Or I'll put you to sleep."

"Yes, my goddess," he said and then ducked when she swatted at him.

7

AN UNFAMILIAR LESSON
(92 TRALONGS)

"**A**FTER OUR RECENT EXPERIENCE," Tseluna said. "I think we should work on your obedience."

"I already promised, didn't I?" Rory said, looking down and scuffing his feet.

"You did," she said. "But I still think we should practice. As my familiar, you should act without thinking when I give you direction."

"That's what I was doing when I went to save Aimee," Rory said, sullenly.

"Yes, but you weren't doing it because I told you to," Tseluna chided. "I want to train you to obey me without thinking when I give you an order."

"It doesn't seem like a very good idea to me," Rory muttered.

"Hey!" Tseluna said sharply. Rory looked up. "Who is smarter? You or me?"

"You are," Rory admitted.

"And who has more experience?"

"You do."

"And so, when I tell you to do something, what are you going to do?"

"I will obey."

"You will obey ..."

"I will obey without thinking," he barked.

"Okay!" she said, clapping her hands. "That's what I wanted to hear. Now, drop and give me 20 push-ups!"

"What! Why?" he said. Tseluna just looked at him reproachfully. He turned bright red, sighed, and dropped to the ground and did 20 pushups.

"Let's try this," she said. Rory closed his eyes and found that he couldn't open them.

"Aaah! What are you doing?" he said in a panic.

"Ssh!" Tseluna said. "I'm going to take you somewhere you can practice."

Rory felt the now familiar change of teleportation and the air smelled different. There was a slight breeze coming from a different direction. He could hear waves crashing on a shore, but they sounded distant, like they were far below. He could hear the cries of seagulls.

"You're on the wall of an ancient castle," she said. "High above the rocks at the coast. The wall is only a couple of feet wide. I'm going to tell you how to cross so you don't fall. It's a long way down, so listen carefully."

Rory could feel himself begin to sweat.

"Turn right about forty degrees," Tseluna said. "A little more. Perfect. Now take four steps forward."

Rory complied, his skin prickling with fear.

"How far down is it?" he asked.

"It's only 100 feet on the left," Tseluna said. "But it's about 500 feet on the right. Now, there's a gap in front of you, so you need to jump about two feet. Don't jump too far because there's another gap ahead. Now jump!"

Rory screwed up his courage and jumped. When he landed, he almost lost his balance and teetered on one foot for a moment, arms cartwheeling, but then got square on the balls of his feet, hyperventilating.

"This is scary," he said, in a panicky voice. "Can we stop now? I get it. I'll listen carefully and obey promptly from now on."

"Not quite yet," Tseluna said. "We need to get you the rest of the way across."

"How much farther is it?"

"Oh, it's a ways," she chuckled. "Take two steps forward. A little more—shuffle forward maybe six inches. Good. Now jump again, just like last time."

Rory jumped again and landed more firmly as he got better at managing his balance without his eyesight.

"Good boy!" she said. "Now walk straight ahead slowly for about ten steps but stop when I tell you to stop."

He took deliberate, slow steps and counted them: one, two, three, until he got to 8 when she told him to stop.

"Turn left. A little more. Now inch forward six inches. Jump again—just like before."

Rory was beginning to pant with the strain, but he jumped and landed securely.

"Now walk straight ahead."

"How far?"

"Walk straight ahead, I said," she chided. He took deliberate steps, waiting for her to stop him. He almost stumbled when he stepped from one surface to another. He'd been walking on some hard flat surface and then found himself on grass. Then he bumped into Tseluna who patted him on the head and let him open his eyes.

She turned him around. They were on a high cliff over the ocean and there was a ruined stone structure that was aligned with the top that had just the tops of the walls remaining. She had walked him around the perimeter of the top, jumping over gaps and crenelations.

She put her arms around him and whispered in his ear, "Let's practice a little more someplace else." She created a portal and reached her hand out to him. He looked through the portal but couldn't make sense of what he was seeing.

"Why do you have to hold my hand when we go through a dimensional portal?"

"To protect the familiar bond," Tseluna said. "As long as we're in the same dimension, I can just teleport you and we'll stay connected. But if I were to leave the dimension without you … Well, it would be bad."

Rory swallowed.

"Would it kill me?"

"Oh, probably not *that* bad," she clarified. "It would just be inconvenient because I'd have to find you and catch you again."

"But … But I want to be caught!"

"Come on, Sugar," she said, taking his hand and leading him through.

Rory had never experienced such a shock before. They stepped out of a small alley and were in a city, but a city the scale of which Rory had neither witnessed nor imagined. The tallest building he'd ever seen was four or five stories high. But all around him were buildings that must have been tens or hundreds of stories high. They felt like they were leaning over him and he wanted to hide.

On the sidewalk, there were thousands of people streaming in both directions. In the road there were enormous vehicles of all different sizes and descriptions making roaring noises. And he could see what appeared to be winged machines in the air too. He looked around, bug-eyed with shock.

"We're in the largest city in Japan. I want you to follow me and stay exactly two paces back," she said. "If I stop, you stop. If I turn, you turn."

"Yes, Tseluna."

She started walking and Rory followed. She turned left at one intersection and walked down an even larger, busier street until they reached a truly enormous intersection. Vast numbers of people were waiting but then started to walk

when an audible signal went off. Rory looked around and when he looked back Tseluna was gone.

In a panic, Rory looked around trying to find her when she poked him in the back with her finger and gave him a nasty shock.

"Ow! What was that for?" he said, rubbing his shoulder.

"Stay focused," she said. "I told you to follow me—not look around."

They waited through the next cycle of the intersection and crossed. Tseluna led him up and then turned off into an arcade of intersecting alleyways with storefronts with red lanterns. Rory tried to carefully stay focused on Tseluna but wanted to look around too. There were interesting smells of unfamiliar food, they went by one place where, through the door, Rory caught a glimpse of a girl performing some kind of erotic dance which captured his attention for a moment until he got shocked again.

"Focus!" Tseluna chided him.

Rory started to answer, but then started to feel vague and confused. He staggered.

"What were we doing again?"

Tseluna looked at him, then pulled him close and touched her forehead to his.

"You've got a fever," she said. "No wonder you're out of sorts. You're getting sick."

"Can you fix it?" Rory asked.

"If we had no other choice, I might try," she said. "But I think we should just take you home and put you to bed."

She opened the portal and led him back into his bedroom. She directed him to remove his clothes and get under the covers.

"In a little bit, I'll make you something to eat. In Japan, they make rice porridge. But in other places they make chicken soup for people who are sick. Do you have a preference?"

"Chicken soup sounds good," he said, with his teeth chattering. She climbed into bed with him and warmed him up for a few minutes while she stroked his brow. He fell into a fitful sleep.

Tseluna went out to the kitchen and found sufficient ingredients to make a simple chicken-noodle soup. As she was finishing up, Rory's dad came home. Tseluna, in the guise of Mrs. T, told him about Rory's fever.

"Rory's sick?" he said. "Thank you for taking care of him, Mrs. T!"

"It's my pleasure," she said, with a smile. "I enjoy working with him every day."

"To be honest," Rory's dad said. "Since his mom died, Rory's been really depressed. He basically hasn't had much interest in anything since. It's been wonderful to see how he's taken to this scholarship. I can't remember the last time he's seemed so happy. Thank you!"

Tseluna smiled and carried a bowl of soup back to Rory's bedroom.

Rory was awake.

"Did I hear my dad come home?"

"Yes," Tseluna said. "I have some dinner for you."

She set it down, then lifted Rory up and folded a pillow behind him. She picked up the bowl and offered to feed him.

"I can feed myself," he said, blushing. He accepted the bowl and spoon and began to eat.

"It's good!" he said. "How did you learn to cook?"

"If you really want to know, I've learned to cook with people at a number of points in time. When I first began to interact with people, they were cooking on sticks over fires or burying pots in coals. But I've also completed several courses of study in cooking, some at prestigious institutions. And, of course, I've just cooked a lot for people over time."

"How long have you been ... What did you say? Interacting with people?"

"Um. I guess it's been a few million tralongs," she said.

"How many tralongs in a year? 500?" he asked, his eyes widening as he made the mental calculation.

"Yeah. Roughly."

"How old are you exactly?" Rory asked.

"A lady never tells," Tseluna said, turning her head primly to the side.

Rory finished his bowl of soup. Tseluna felt his forehead.

"Your fever is lower," she said. "Why don't you take a shower and I'll change your sheets. These are soaked."

Rory crossed the hall to the bathroom in the nude. His dad spotted him and said, "Hey! There's a lady in the house, young man!"

"She's my coach, dad!" Rory called, as he started the shower.

Rory's dad came down the hall and saw Tseluna stripping the mattress.

"I'm sorry he's … Oh, you don't have to do that!" he said.

"It's no problem, Mr. Soletsa," she said. "Making sure he gets enough rest is an important part of coaching."

She made the bed and, when Rory came back in, all warm from the shower, she turned the covers back and tucked him in.

"Thank you," he said.

"Need anything else?"

"Would you … Would you please hold my hand?"

Tseluna took his hand in hers and patted him gently through the covers until he fell back asleep.

•   •   •

The next morning he had received special dispensation from Tseluna to not go running while he convalesced and was therefore able to linger at breakfast with his dad. His dad remarked on how impressed he was with Mrs. T as a coach— and as a woman.

"She's very attractive," his dad said. "She speaks well and is kind of exotic-looking. Do you know where she's from?"

"Dad, she's not even …" he started to say without thinking when suddenly his throat closed up when he tried to say the word "human" and he began to strangle.

"Ah, ah, ah!" he heard in his head. "Let's not say that. Just say something nice and neutral."

Suddenly, he could breathe again. He gasped in a big lungful of air.

"Yeah, I don't know where she's from," he concluded.

"Good boy!" she said in his head and he felt the customary little nudge of pleasure.

8

FAMILIAR DAYS
(N TRALONGS)

AFTER HE RECOVERED from his fever, Rory and Tseluna settled into a regular routine. At 5am, Rory awoke to find Tseluna presenting a breast to him. He nursed on first one side and then the other. By 5:15, she broke his latch and made him get up. While he pulled on his running shorts, she teleported outside the house and rang the doorbell. He ran out to the breezeway to answer the door. While Rory put his shoes on, Rory's dad frequently came out for a few minutes to have small talk with Tseluna in her guise as Mrs. T. Then they headed out for their morning run.

At first, Tseluna let Rory set the pace until he was warmed up. Afterward, she ran just behind him and, if he slowed down enough to let her get within reach, she would touch him with a finger and give him a painful shock. Once had been enough to convince him to never want to let that happen again and he picked up the pace to stay ahead of her.

They typically followed the same route that ran far off into the country before turning right and making a wide circuit, returning to town from another direction all together. In the last mile before getting home, Tseluna would suddenly sprint to catch up with Rory and he needed to give it everything he had to stay ahead of her to avoid getting shocked. When they reached the last street, she let him slow to a walk to cool down before reaching the house.

By the time they got home, Rory's dad had already left for work, so they arrived to an empty house. Rory went to shower and change while Tseluna fixed him a large breakfast of toast, eggs, and sausage or bacon.

After breakfast, they went into the back yard, where Tseluna led Rory in a long period of stretching followed by quiet meditation in *seiza* position. After three hours of solid activity, Rory found the meditation relaxing and peaceful, but in spite of Tseluna looking completely asleep, she was continuously monitoring Rory and if his mind started to wander, or if he started to fantasize or fall asleep, she would painfully pinch him somewhere. She could somehow do this while appearing utterly quiescent. And Rory would curse and try to stay focused on his meditation without becoming distracted.

After meditation, they spent two hours practicing aikido. They would vary between moving through forms, practicing particular techniques, and sparring. Rory was unable to lay a hand on Tseluna, who could throw him or push him off balance seemingly without effort.

"You're cheating," he finally said, while picking himself up off the ground. "You've got to be cheating."

"We can go back to Japan and you can try against Hideyoshi-san again."

Rory mumbled curses and tried again. And again.

Shortly before noon, they went back inside and Rory fixed lunch for them to carry out. Then Tseluna would put a hand on his shoulder and teleport them to some remote, unpeopled location where they could practice dangerous magic without worrying about injuring innocent bystanders.

The afternoon was spent with Tseluna tutoring Rory in defensive and offensive spells. She had tried to teach him to activate spells without speaking a word of power, but he had thus far been unable to make it work.

"It's just a bad habit," she said. "It's totally unnecessary and it slows you down."

"It just doesn't work if I don't say it," he said.

"Okay," she said. "Let's try this." She gestured at him and he found that he was mute. He couldn't say anything. He opened and closed his mouth like a fish trying to emit a sound.

She walked slowly toward him with a finger extended.

"You'd better raise your shield or you're going to get such a shock!" she said, with a wicked grin.

She moved forward at a deliberate pace. He tried desperately to say the word, to think the word, to mouth the word …

"What's wrong?" she chuckled malevolently. "Cat got your tongue?"

Her finger grew closer and closer. Sweat broke out on his forehead.

"Where do you want it?" she said, pointing her finger at various sensitive locations. "Here? Here? Or here!"

Her finger was touching his shirt and he was bracing himself for the inevitable shock, when something clicked—like moving a muscle you didn't know you had—and his shield activated, pushing her finger back.

Tseluna unmuted him and gently patted him on the head. "Good boy!"

He grinned, well-pleased with his accomplishment.

Tseluna also began to teach him a whole variety of enhancements to his basic shield spell to strengthen it for various kinds of attacks. He could tune it for temperature, kinetic, and other kinds of forces to maximize its effectiveness.

She also tried to teach him to maintain his shield while casting other spells, to extend his shield out from his body, and to cast it around other objects, but these proved too difficult and he was unable to make any immediate progress.

She also taught him a variety of offensive techniques. He learned how to cast magic missiles and windblades. And they continued to develop his ability to use magic to apply force to objects: to push, pull, and pick things up.

"Can you teach me to teleport?" Rory asked.

"That's not a good idea," she said to his great disappointment. "Yet. We'll see if we get there. But it's way too easy to teleport yourself up in the air or under ground. The most important thing for you to work on is your shield. Until you can really control your shield, you're a sitting duck."

Finally, as the sun was setting, Tseluna teleported them back home where she resumed her role as a kitten and Rory had dinner alone with his father. His father was always very pleased to hear about his various adventures and how much he was learning, although Rory found that Tseluna set tight restrictions on how much information he could reveal regarding his new capabilities.

Once he had his summer homework completed, Tseluna allowed him two hours in the evening to use as he wanted, to read, or play a game, or take a walk. And then she insisted he go to bed by 9pm. After he got into bed, she sometimes climbed in with him to cuddle. But frequently, he was already asleep.

He had never been so busy or so tired or so happy.

9

FAMILIAR ELEMENTALS

(81 TRALONGS)

"ELEMENTALS SURE ARE CONVENIENT," Rory said, turning out the elemental lights and getting into bed after a long day of training.

"Convenient? Have you never caught elementals before?" Tseluna asked.

"Huh?" Rory said, surprised. "What?"

"Oh! C'mon! Let's go!"

For a moment, as exhausted as he was, Rory was torn between just staying in bed and going to sleep and staying up later to go on an adventure. But adventure beckoned—plus he knew that Tseluna would probably zap him if he didn't obey promptly—so he bounced back out of bed and got dressed again.

He opened the door to his room and met his father coming out of the bathroom.

"Where are you going at this hour?" he asked.

"Oh, uh ..." he stammered. And then Tseluna took over his mouth. "Mrs. T invited me to meet her at the park tonight because she says the wild elementals are pretty and I shouldn't miss seeing them."

"Oh," he said. "Well, if Mrs. T says to go then you should go and not keep her waiting, don't you think?"

"Yes, Dad," Rory said and started to head out.

"Wait. You need to grab some salt," Tseluna, now in kitten form, subvocalized to him.

"How much do we need?" Rory asked.

"A goodly amount."

Rory went into the kitchen and found that there was a new, unopened package of salt in the cabinet. He snagged it and carried it with him out of the house. He had barely set foot outside when he felt the shift of teleportation and he found himself standing next to Tseluna, now in her usual form, in the middle of a grassland that extended as far as the eye could see in every direction.

The first thing he noticed was the sky. It had never looked so clear and full of stars before. He looked up and turned around and around looking at the heavens.

"It's beautiful," he said, stunned.

"It is, isn't it," Tseluna said, glancing up. "Can you see the Sky Foam?"

"What's that?" Rory asked.

"Stars are organized into galaxies, which are like flat spirals. But since we're inside looking out, you can see the edge of the spiral and looking in, you can see the middle plus the spiral. There! See there? That band that looks like clouds? People here call that Sky Foam."

"It's amazing."

"Now look down."

Rory looked around and realized he could see little sparks of light moving among the grasses in the dark.

"Are those all elementals?" he asked.

"Yep. An undisturbed natural area like this will typically have the highest concentration of wild elementals."

"How do we catch them?"

"We need to construct a trap. For that, we need to dig a little trench."

"How can we do that? We don't have a shovel and the grass is really high."

Tseluna gestured and a 10-foot by 10-foot section of sod lifted up and moved to the side. Underneath, an assortment of worms and grubs writhed to be suddenly exposed.

"Use your finger and make a groove in a big circle."

She stood in the middle. Rory squatted down and carefully inscribed a circle in the soft black soil.

"Now pour a line of salt in the groove all the way around. You don't need to fill it with salt—just enough to make a connection."

She supervised while Rory opened the package of salt and poured it carefully into the groove. He went all the way around her.

"Salt circles make a simple barrier if you invest them with a little magical energy. Some elements can make stronger barriers like silver and mercury. But salt is cheap and easy to work with. Touch your finger to the salt and push in a little magical energy."

Rory complied and he could feel when the circle activated.

"But how do the elementals get inside?" he asked.

"Ah! You're a bit ahead of yourself. This is just a circle. If an elemental were inside now, it couldn't get out. But you're right—they can't get inside either.

"Before we make the trap, though, experiment with the circle for a minute. First, does the circle stop you?"

Rory stuck his hand into the area enclosed by the circle.

"Nope."

"Can you feel anything?"

Rory put his hand in more slowly this time.

"Maybe? I can maybe feel something. But it's pretty minimal."

"Watch this," she said. She reached a hand out and it stopped at the barrier. She pushed harder and demonstrated that she could not reach outside.

"You really can't get out?"

"Not as such. Magical creatures are blocked by this kind of barrier. The easiest way for me to get out is simply to disrupt the salt and break the circle," she said, gesturing at the circle and a little puff of air brushed away two inches of the salt. Rory could feel that the barrier was gone and Tseluna stepped out.

"Now, let's make a trap. The first thing we need to add is an immersion."

"Immersion? What does that word mean?" Rory asked.

"Oh. It's how we represent an entrance that passes through an extra dimension to bypass the circle. You can draw it like this," she used a finger to sketch a complex shape where she had created the opening. "Go ahead and add the salt."

"It goes through another dimension? Like Japan?"

"Oh. No. Different kind of dimension. You need a fourth dimension, in addition to our regular three, for the lines to not intersect."

"I don't understand."

"I can show you the math later, but for now, just take my word for it and add the salt."

Rory complied. He messed up one spot where he had added too much salt. Tseluna gestured and the salt was gone in that area and Rory tried a second time to master the eldritch shape with delicate lines of salt.

"Good! That's good!" she said. "Now, we need to add the bait. Make two little piles of salt here and here." Rory did as she directed.

"Now, you need to invest the trap with magical energy and then do the same with the bait."

Rory felt the trap activate when he pushed some magical power into the circle. Then he reached his hand in and powered up the bait. As soon as he did, elementals began streaking in from all directions.

"Whoa!" Rory said, stepping back.

The elementals would bump up against the barrier, then follow it around until they reached the immersion and then pass into the inside of the trap. He tried to count at first, but there were too many. At first there were dozens, but they kept coming and within just a few minutes, the trap was seething with hundreds or thousands of elementals.

"Wow. That's a lot of elementals," Rory said. "Should we do anything with them?"

"Elementals are useful for many purposes," Tseluna said. "The technology here is almost entirely elemental based: refrigerators, hot water heaters, lights, etc. But using wild elementals requires sorting them by type and training them, so it's easier to just buy the right ones. But it's always nice to know where things come from, how they work, and that we could do it ourselves, if we really wanted to."

"So should we just let them go?"

"Sure," she said.

Rory ran his finger through the salt circle and he felt the spell fall apart. Suddenly the elementals, freed from their constraint, flashed off in every direction. Rory laughed as some bumped into him and got caught in his shirt.

"That tickles!" he tittered as they zipped around trying to get out of his shirt.

Once the elementals had dispersed, Tseluna lifted the sod she had removed earlier and replaced it. Then she teleported them back home.

Rory fell asleep the moment his head hit his pillow. He dreamed of elementals flying among the stars.

10

AN UNFAMILIAR GAME
(73 TRALONGS)

"HEY, TSELUNA," RORY BEGAN. "Usually on Wednesdays, I have game night with my friends."

"And you want to play 'Demon Quest' with your friends tonight?"

Rory looked at her hopefully.

"Can I play too?"

"You want to play?" he said, in shock. "A girl? And aren't you a little too old to play?"

Tseluna transformed, like she had at the festival, into a young, black woman who looked about Rory's age, wearing an unfamiliar school uniform. She twirled around, lifting her skirt.

"But do you even know how to play?" Rory asked.

Tseluna put her hands on her hips and just stared at him.

"Oh, right. You can just refer to my memories can't you?"

"Well? Are you ready?" Tseluna transformed back into a kitten and hopped up on Rory's shoulder.

Rory grimaced, worried about what the other boys would say. He grabbed his bag where he kept all his game stuff, said goodbye to his dad, and they headed out.

"How should I introduce you?" Rory subvocalized to Tseluna.

"Why don't you call me Sunny."

"And your—heh—'demon name'?"

"How about Lady SunBlade."

By the time they arrived at Robert and Gabe's house, Tseluna had transformed again. Rory knocked and Gabe opened the door to them. Gabe was the same age as Rory with brown skin and dark, frizzy hair.

"Hey, Rory! We weren't sure you were going to be able to make it!"

"Yeah, I've been pretty busy. I was telling my friend Sunny about our game and she wanted to come try."

Gabe looked sidelong at Rory who just blinked absently and pretended he didn't notice.

"Okay. You can head on down," Gabe said.

Gabe stayed to greet the others at the door while Rory and Tseluna went down into the basement where Gabe's older brother Robert was setting up at the big, round table they used for playing Demon Quest. Robert, who looked like a larger, broader version of his brother Gabe, was two years older than the other boys and had a crow as a familiar.

"Well met, Your Highness," Rory said to Robert, following the Protocol.

"Well met, Lord RazorFell."

"Sire, may I introduce Lady SunBlade?"

"How do you do, Lady SunBlade," His Majesty said, inclining his head.

"By your grace, Your Highness," Tseluna said, curtsying. The Protocol was unclear what a girl was supposed to do since no girl had ever attended game night before. But a boy was supposed to bow and so she figured a curtsy was the appropriate move. Rory and Robert were both extremely impressed and it showed on their faces.

Next, Rory stepped to the basement fridge, which was always stocked with plenty of drinks for game night.

"Do you want something to drink?" he asked Tseluna.

"Do they have milk?"

"They do!" Rory said, handing her a bottle. He selected a bottle of juice for himself. Then they found seats at the table and he got out his dice and character sheets.

"Sire, may I petition thee for a character sheet?" Lady SunBlade said.

"As you wish, Lady SunBlade," His Majesty said, handing her a sheet of paper. "Roll four dice and take the highest three."

As she was rolling her character, Lord LightStrike (aka Larry) and Lord FrostFire (aka Fred) arrived. Then Lord DarkSoul (aka Dan) came in followed by Lord GapTongue (aka Gabe, Robert's little brother) who came last, once all of the anticipated guests had arrived.

"Welcome, my Lords! And Lady!" His Majesty intoned. "Tonight, we continue our Demon Quest through the Arms of Falls Hallow.

"We begin where we left off last time. You're standing on a low cliff overlooking the Valley of Smoke. Lady SunBlade arrives from the south."

"What are you, Lady SunBlade?" asked Lord GapTongue.

"I'm a human mage, Milord!" she said.

"What does the party want to do?" His Majesty asked.

"We should head into the valley," Lord LightStrike said.

"Do you want to head straight into the valley?" His Majesty asked.

"I think we should look for a path down first," Lord RazorFell said.

"Rather than jumping to your deaths, you follow Lord RazorFell who scouts along the edge of the cliff until you find a trail that leads down."

"Larry is about to say something stupid," Tseluna subvocalized to Rory.

"That's why the girls all call him Larry the Loser," Rory asked back. "Do you want me to do something?"

"Thank you, but I can take care of it," she replied.

"I'm going to follow Lady SunBlade," Lord LightStrike said. "And flip her skirt up to see what color panties she's wearing."

"When he does that, Sire, I'm going to trip him while he's distracted," Lady Sunblade said.

"Roll under your dexterities," His Majesty said. Lord LightStrike rolled a natural twenty and Lady SunBlade rolled a one. "Lord LightStrike needed to roll under his dexterity to flip the skirt, but he blew it spectacularly. Instead, he tripped over his scabbard and fell. And Lady SunBlade needed to roll under her dexterity plus 2—due to his distraction—to trip Lord LightStrike. She succeeded beyond her wildest dreams and when Lord LightStrike fell, he hit his head on her boot and took … 4 points of damage. He does not succeed in observing Lady SunBlade's panties.

"And Larry?" Robert said, breaking character. "Don't be a creep."

"Hehehe," Lord LightStrike tittered, but kind of trailed off when it became clear that everyone else was just staring at him.

"What can we see when we get into the valley?" Lord RazorFell asked.

"Everyone roll under their wisdom."

Everyone rolled. Everyone blew their rolls but Lord DarkSoul who got a two.

"Wh-what d-d-do I s-s-see?" he asked.

"You hear the sound of marching feet approaching from the south."

Everyone waited, looking at Lord DarkSoul expectantly.

"Uh … I hear m-m-marching feet."

Lady SunBlade began barking orders: "GapTongue, LightStrike! As fighters without ranged weapons, you must hold the bottom of the trail and fall back as necessary. RazorFell, FrostFire, DarkSoul, go back up the trail to the first switchback, and use ranged attacks once the enemy force comes into view. I will stand in between to relay communications between the parties and back-up the melee fighters."

"Is that what the party wants to do?" His Majesty asked.

"I follow the orders of Lady SunBlade," Lord RazorFell said.

"Me too! Me too!" said the others except for Larry.

"I think we should charge them," Lord LightStrike said.

"Th-they're m-m-marching," Lord DarkSoul said. "Th-that s-s-suggests th-they're w-well t-trained."

"And soldiers wouldn't march unless they had a leader," Lady SunBlade said. "So, they'll probably get a leadership bonus."

"Just follow orders," said Lord FrostFire, who had been quiet up till now.

"Hey! Who put the girl in command?" Lord LightStrike said.

"While you're arguing," His Majesty said. "The sound of marching is getting closer. You are unable to accurately estimate the number, but you can hear someone giving orders and you determine that they are goblins."

"I ignore Lord LightStrike and take my assigned position," Lord RazorFell said. "I am scanning carefully for any sighting of the enemy and plan to attack as soon as I can identify a target."

"Me too! Me too!" said the others.

"Roll wisdom again for perception." This time they did better and Lords RazorFell, FrostFire, and DarkSoul all rolled low numbers.

"You can see the force," His Majesty said.

"I'm going to—" Lord FrostFire started to say.

"Wait!" Lady SunBlade said. "Wait until you can identify the leader and then you all attack that one."

"Can we tell which one is the leader, Sire?" asked Lord RazorFell. His Majesty rolled a die.

"Yes. You can tell which one is the leader."

"We all attack that one."

Their ranged attacks were successful at bringing down the leader, so it was a mob that attacked the fighters at the bottom of the trail. With the support of Lady SunBlade, they repelled the small force. And, with that, Tseluna became the *de facto* leader of the party.

They played for several hours and made good progress, eventually finding the entrance to the dungeon. Around then, Lord GapTongue started falling asleep and they wrapped up for the night.

"It was very nice to meet you, Lady SunBlade," His Majesty said, inclining his head. "Thank you for coming!"

"By your grace, Sire," she said with another curtsy that made all the boys look at Rory enviously. Rory packed up his stuff and they headed out into the night.

"You're really very good at small-unit tactics," Rory said as they walked home.

"You have nice friends," she said.

"Except for Larry the Loser."

"Oh, he's not that bad. He just says out loud what the rest of them are only thinking. I know how boys are. C'mon. Admit it. You wanted to know what color they are too."

"Were you reading their minds?"

"Only a little. And I didn't cheat," she said, looking him in the eye. "I didn't read the Game Master at all. But I did peek at people in the party to know the capabilities of their characters. You don't keep track of that very well. That's key to being an effective leader."

"You did a nice job pushing back on Larry when he tried to look at your panties. You played it just right and got everyone on your side."

"Praise me more," Tseluna said, grinning. "And we'll do game night again next week."

11

A FAMILIAR ENIGMA
(67 TRALONGS)

R ORY WAS HEADED THROUGH TOWN in the early morning when he noticed something. There was someone moving around inside a closed business. He ran on past without giving any sign he'd seen anything, but then he turned off at the next street and slipped into the alley along the back of the businesses.

"Why have you stopped running?" Tseluna said sharply in his head.

"I thought I saw something suspicious," he thought back. He got her mental eyeroll, but she let him continue.

When he got to the next building, he listened as he approached the back door which was standing ajar. The business had been closed for months. He knew this could just be something totally innocent, but it didn't feel like that. He heard the sound of someone chopping or banging something, which reinforced his sense of unease. Then Rory noticed that the business next door was a jewelry store. He put two and two together and had a pretty good idea of what was going on.

He hung back while the banging continued but, after a few minutes, the banging stopped. Then Rory slipped into the closed store, which was dark after the bright morning sky. He stood for a minute letting his eyes adjust. He was standing in a kind of stockroom. It had empty shelves with a few empty boxes on the floor. Everything was covered with dust. He pressed deeper into the store.

When he peeked through the door into the front, he found that the thief had broken a hole through the wall and into the adjacent business. He was kneeling by a safe and had attached some kind of listening device to it. He was entirely focused on listening while turning the dial and didn't notice Rory peeking in at him. Rory considered what to do and remembered the sleep spell Tseluna had taught him. He organized his thoughts, collected a tiny bit of power, and then reached out and stroked the thief's hypothalamus. The thief slumped over.

Rory took a leisurely jog over to the constabulary.

"Excuse me," he said to the man at the front desk. "I thought I saw someone breaking into the jewelry store on Main Street."

The man assigned a couple of constables to investigate. Rory led them over and pointed through the window, where the man's slumped position was just barely visible.

At that moment, the business owner arrived and was able to open the door for the deputies. They apprehended the thief. He awoke blearily as he was being handcuffed and looked around uncomprehendingly.

"Ugh," the jewelry store owner said. "He's with that gang of thugs that's been trying to make me pay protection money." He turned to Rory. "Thank you very much, young man. But you should be careful—I hope they don't take any interest in you."

"Good boy," Tseluna said, in his head. And he felt the customary little bump of pleasure.

Rory grinned, chuffed to have been of service, and then headed back out to finish his run.

•   •   •

After three hours of aikido practice and then lunch, rather than taking him to some remote location, Tseluna merely led Rory back out into the backyard.

"Today we're going to learn something new," Tseluna said.

"Is it more powerful than fireballs?" Rory asked, rubbing his hands.

Tseluna cocked her head over while she considered.

"Well," she said. "Just like with fireballs, the power is only limited by how much power you put into it."

"Alright!"

"This is a force called 'electricity'," she explained. "It's the same kind of power you see with lightning."

"Wow," Rory gushed. "Now that's powerful!"

"But it's a lot more versatile than that," she continued. "Like this!" And she touched his shoulder with her finger and zapped him so he got the nasty shock like she been giving him when he misbehaved.

"Ow! What was that for?"

"To get your head away from the idea that raw power is the most important thing. This is not a dick-measuring contest."

Crestfallen, his ears colored.

"Electricity is an incredibly useful form of energy. Your body uses electricity to send messages. And in Japan they use electricity to make lights work and to heat stuff and to do many other useful things."

"Lights? Heat? Don't they use elementals?"

"No magic," she said. "Remember? No elementals either."

"Whoa," Rory said, mind blown. "I just can't even picture how that works."

"Electricity flows. Very simply, it flows from high to low—which is usually the ground."

"You mean, it only flows downhill, like water?"

"Not exactly. It flows from high concentration to low. You can create an artificial low concentration and then the electricity will flow from the ground to that. It also flows through some materials more easily than others. It particularly likes metals. And water. Well, water with dissolved ions."

"Huh?"

"Never mind," she said, shaking her head. "We're getting off in the weeds. Here. Watch!"

She showed him how she could gather power and then use it to generate an electrical charge around her hand. When she moved it toward the tree, a bright spark jumped from her hand to the tree and tore a jagged line through the bark to the ground as the water in the sap flashed to steam.

"But you need to be able to keep your shield up while you cast the spell so you don't zap yourself. And be careful around other people too. They're bags of mostly water and you'll kill them if you zap them very hard."

"But I can't do that," Rory said. "My shield doesn't stay up when I cast another spell."

"You can do it," Tseluna said, patting him on his head. "You just haven't quite figured it out yet. Have you tried again since you figured out how to silently cast spells? Try something simple and safe. Try to make a light."

Rory raised his shield. When he went to make a light, he spoke the word of power out of habit, and his shield dropped.

"Sorry."

"Try again," she said, exasperated.

He raised his shield again and then silently triggered the light spell. This time, his shield did not drop.

"It worked!" he marveled. "It really worked!"

"Well done!" she said, hugging him. "You did it!"

He beamed with pleasure at his success and being praised.

"Note that you can also use electricity through metal or water to zap enemies. Here. Come over here and zap this clothesline pole to practice, so we don't damage the tree any more than necessary. But be very careful with your shield: if you zap yourself, it can be very dangerous—even deadly."

Rory carefully used only a small amount of power at first and made just tiny blue sparks. Gradually he turned up the power making larger and larger sparks.

"Can I try a really strong one?" he asked.

"You'd better not," she said. "We don't want to damage the clothesline. And if they get much larger, they'll make a lot of noise and light, which might attract unwanted attention. Some time, we'll go somewhere else so you can cast a really big one."

•　　　•　　　•

After dinner, Rory was lounging with Tseluna in bed reading a graphic novel during his free time. He came to a stopping off point and thought of something.

"Hey, Mommy! Can we ..." Rory began and then realized what he had said. His eyes sprang open as he discovered that Tseluna and his mother were coming to occupy the same place in his mind. He suddenly found himself filled with rage and anguish.

"No! No!" he hissed, tears suddenly streaming down his face. "You're not my mother! You can't become my mother! What are you doing?"

He pushed her away then flipped over in the bed and curled up against the wall weeping.

She waited, silently, while he cried himself out. They laid there for a long time with a distance between them.

"What's happening to me?" he said, finally, in a tiny voice.

"You're becoming my familiar," Tseluna said. "This kind of transference isn't unusual."

"Does it ever get better? Does this ... pain ever go away?"

"Well, you aren't going to live forever," she countered. This struck him as hysterically funny and he began to laugh. He turned over and hugged Tseluna.

"Thank you, Mommy," he said.

"*Baka!*" she replied. "Don't push it."

12

AN UNFAMILIAR SHOCK

(58 TRALONGS)

ON HIS EARLY MORNING RUN, Rory got the feeling he was being followed. He couldn't see anyone behind him, but he had a niggling feeling that he couldn't shake. So, he decided to pick up the pace. He extended his gait and put some additional distance between himself and whoever might be behind him.

"Is everything okay?" Tseluna said to him, sleepily. She'd been staying in bed lately and monitoring his performance remotely. She claimed she didn't need to sleep, but Rory was becoming unconvinced.

"Probably," he said. "But I might have someone on my tail."

"As long as you're where no one can see you, you can take care of them however you see fit," Tseluna said.

Rory grinned to himself.

In the middle of the forest, there was the long metal suspension bridge that carried the trail over the muddy stream. Rory started on one side and got to the middle when he realized there was someone standing on the far side blocking the path. When he looked back, he saw there was someone at the other end as well. They had chosen a good place for the ambush, as he was caught between with no obvious way to escape. He slowed to a walk while he considered what to do. They closed in on him from both directions.

Since the bridge was made of metal, he decided that he'd try using the electricity spell that Tseluna had taught him. He raised his shield, grasped the rails of the bridge, organized his mind, and then marshaled as much power as he could. He nearly spoke a word of power, but remembered in time and he triggered the spell silently. There was a loud popping noise and suddenly the bridge began throwing off bright sparks along its entire length. The two men went rigid and started smoking as they were electrocuted. But then the whole bridge glowed red with heat. Some of the structural elements glowed even hotter, fatigued, and, with a screech, the entire bridge collapsed into the stream, dumping Rory and the two corpses into the muddy water with a hiss.

Rory dragged himself, uninjured, from the stinking mire. He could sense Tseluna's amusement.

"Don't say it," Rory said. "Just ... don't say anything."

Rory squelched his way home, attracting stares, totally covered in mud. When he finally arrived home, he stepped in the front door and, no sooner had he closed the door, but Tseluna teleported him directly into the shower, leaving his muddy clothes behind. He turned the water on and watched the mud sluice off his body and run down the drain.

After he emerged from the shower, he was drying off and caught a glimpse of himself in the mirror. Then he turned and looked more carefully. He'd put on an astonishing amount of lean muscle. Where he had been rangy before, he now looked like a bodybuilder, with powerful, sculpted muscles. Fascinated, he struck a few poses and then felt his biceps. Suddenly, he felt another pair of hands on his body.

"Ooh," Tseluna said, running her hands over his shoulders and arms. "Let me get some of this too!"

She pulled him into an embrace and kissed him roughly. He returned her kiss, pulling her to him, but with one eye still turned toward the mirror.

•　　•　　•

After aikido practice and lunch, Tseluna took Rory again into the backyard rather than teleporting them to some remote location to practice.

"What's up?" he asked.

"This afternoon," Tseluna said, in *seiza* position. "I want you to learn to resist mind probes."

"Doesn't the familiar bond just let you do that to me?"

"Well, yeah. Now. But I was reading your mind well before then. You people have basically no resistance. I want you to learn to recognize when you're being mind-probed and to put up some resistance. I don't know how likely it is that it will happen during the tournament, but it's just good practice."

She warned him and then cut off his access to the familiar bond. It felt strange and uncomfortable to be alone in his own head. Then she led him through recognizing the characteristics of being mind-probed. It wasn't anything definite, but he could feel a sense of uneasiness and a sense of being watched—almost like someone was looking over his shoulder. He was reminded of how he felt when he first encountered Tseluna as a kitten in the park. Next, she taught him techniques to wall off his thoughts from an invader.

"All right," she said, rubbing her hands together. "Are you ready?" Rory nodded.

He felt her invade his mind. This time, however, it was not gently and tentatively like earlier. This was aggressive and forceful. He felt like he was small and exposed before her. He tried desperately to push back without success.

"Well, that didn't go so well," she said. "Let's try again."

But no matter what barriers he tried to erect, he felt her invade his consciousness. And again he was naked before her. She loomed over him in his mind. He gave up as he felt his defenses being overwhelmed.

"Don't stop!" she said, slapping him. "Never surrender! Try harder!"

That shocked him back into action and he pushed back again and harder. He still couldn't stop her from overpowering him, but he did manage to continue to resist.

"That was better," she said. "You'll never be able to stop a determined demon. But if you can at least put up some resistance, they can't take for granted that they can get a good read on your thoughts. And you force them to divide their attention."

"You slapped me," Rory said, holding his hand up to his face.

"Aw ... Here," she said. "Let me kiss it and make it better." She gave him a little kiss on his cheek that made him blush and then she pulled him into an embrace and kissed him on the mouth forcing her rough tongue against his. He wondered abstractly if he ever kissed a girl whether her lack of a rough tongue would mean she could never satisfy him.

•   •   •

That night, Rory was getting ready for bed and realized something.

"You said you can transform yourself to look like pretty much anything, right?"

Tseluna nodded.

"Can you teach me how to transform?" he asked hopefully.

"Sorry," she said, patting his face. "I can transform because I'm a magical creature—I exist separately from the body I construct. You're a biological creature so it doesn't work for you: you *are* your body. You could learn body modification and, say, grow horns. But you'd still have to grow them the old-fashioned way." Rory was crushed.

"I'm just curious," he continued, after a few minutes sulking. "Why do you make your skin so dark?"

"That was actually Hideyoshi-san's idea," Tseluna said. "Here, skin color doesn't really mean anything, right?"

"Mean anything?" Rory said, bewildered by the question. "No, I guess? I mean it's like hair color. Or eye color, right?"

"In Japan," Tseluna said. "There's a lot of prejudice about skin color."

"What? That's stupid!"

"Hideyoshi-san suggested that having me be a dark-skinned woman might help reduce prejudice. And I've just gotten used to it."

"Is there prejudice there about women too?" Rory asked.

"There is," Tseluna said. "Women face discrimination in opportunities, pay, and many other aspects of life."

"Have you ever been a man?" Rory asked. Tseluna nodded.

"Would you like it better if I were a man?" she asked.

"No," Rory said. "I like you fine the way you are."

"I know," she said, grinning. "I read your mind before I presented myself to you, you know. If you were more interested in men, I might have done that."

"What do you look like as a man?" Rory asked, now irrepressibly curious.

Tseluna transformed and Rory looked up in shock at an imposing, naked man more than a foot taller than him—still with bright yellow eyes. Tseluna had sculpted muscles even larger than his and dark hair in braids that hung down to his shoulders. He reached out and gathered Rory into his powerful arms.

"Am I everything you ever dreamed of, Sugar?" Tseluna growled, in a bass rumble.

"I ... I could get used to it," Rory said, coloring. "I love you. And I will love you no matter what you look like. But you can turn back now." After she did, Rory continued. "So, was Hideyoshi-san your familiar too?"

"No, he was never my familiar."

Rory paused, trying to figure out what question to ask next. Tseluna didn't help, so he finally just asked it.

"Was he your boyfriend? Or lover?"

"No," she said. "Hideyoshi-san is … well … He's asexual. He isn't interested in that kind of relationship with anyone. We just became close friends. And partners."

"You mean, you didn't … He didn't …"

"Nope. Never. But he was the one that helped me come up with this current plan."

"He said you saved his life."

"Yes, that was how we met. He was an accountant who discovered that the executives of the firm he was working for were embezzling money from the company. And so he stole all their ill-gotten gains. They caught him, staked him out in the sun, and were withholding water to try to get him to talk. But he knew that as soon as he told them, they'd kill him."

"So how did you get involved?"

"I just happened to pass nearby and I could hear his thoughts. His thoughts were so incredibly clear. It was as though I could hear them even without using a mind probe. Anyway, after I freed him and killed the people who were after him, he insisted on splitting the money with me."

"Do you really need money?"

"No. But it was fun helping him spend it and sharing in his pleasure. He helped me learn more about Japan. And people."

Tseluna raised a finger.

"Now, I believe it's time for a certain young man who doesn't wish to get punished to go to sleep."

13

A FAMILIAR DRAMA

(50 TRALONGS)

A WEEK LATER, RORY AWOKE a bit early one morning and felt grumpy for some reason. Lying abed, he tried to remember going to sleep the night before. He remembered getting into bed, but couldn't remember anything after that. He puzzled about it for a while until Tseluna slipped into bed and presented a breast to him.

"Would you like some nummies?"

"What happened last night when I went to bed?"

"What do you mean?" she said, looking at him with her bright, yellow eyes.

"I just can't remember what happened. I remember getting into bed, but I can't remember anything after that."

"It just seemed ... normal to me," she said.

Rory looked at her and she looked back at him. He became seized with the conviction that she was not being entirely forthcoming.

"What aren't you telling me?" he asked, his eyes narrowing.

"C'mon," she said, offering her breast again. "You need to get started so you can start training."

"No," he said. "You're not telling me something. Did you … do something to me?"

"Like what?"

"Did you put me to sleep?"

"And what if I did?" she said, starting to lose her temper. "You're my familiar. I'll put you to sleep if I want to."

"Fuck that!" he said, angrily. "You need to tell me if you're going to do something like that. And not lie about it afterward."

"C'mon," she said, teasingly, waving her breast at him. "You know you want it."

He flipped himself over, faced the wall, and said, "No."

"Well, if you're not going to, then get up and start running."

"No."

"If you're disobedient, I will punish you."

"No."

She poked him with a finger and zapped him. He grimaced, but laid there without moving.

Suddenly, he found himself getting up against his will. He tried to resist, but his body acted on its own, pulling on his clothes and shoes. He headed out the door and started out on his regular route—against his will.

She ran him into the downtown area and then he felt her withdraw her control. He refused to run and fell on the sidewalk, scraping his knees and forearms. And then he laid there, refusing to move.

Several passers-by rushed over.

"Are you alright, young man? Are you okay?"

He refused to speak and laid there without moving.

"There's something wrong! Someone call for a stretcher!"

Finally, Tseluna took control of him again. She made him get up and start running, leaving the small crowd of people he'd attracted scratching their heads.

By now, Rory was seething and was getting angrier every second and so, a couple of minutes later, when Tseluna relaxed her grip on him for a moment, he suddenly called up magical energy, spoke a word of power, and generated a huge lightning bolt. The flash was blinding, and Rory had never heard something so loud. He was somewhat surprised that he could hear it, since he'd figured it would kill him. But he discovered that Tseluna had somehow managed to bring up his shield before he activated the spell. Then he felt the world shift around him as she teleported him away.

He found himself standing in the middle of a barren plain of sand and rocks. Tseluna was facing him ten feet away with a look of utter fury on her face. They just stood and stared at each other for long seconds

"How dare you!" she hissed, finally. "You nearly killed yourself. Are you trying to find out how badly I can punish you?"

"You can't stop me from killing myself eventually," he said, blood oozing down his arms and legs from his scrapes. "You can't watch me that closely."

They stared daggers at one another for long seconds. Finally, she sighed.

"Is this really so important to you?"

"It's the principle of the thing," he said, squaring his shoulders.

"What is it you want?"

"First, I want you to apologize. Second, I want you to promise you won't do things to me again without telling me. And, finally, I want you to promise to be honest with me and not lie to my face!"

"And if I agree, you'll stop being disobedient?"

"I haven't heard your apology yet."

She looked angrily at him, and he stared back impassively. Finally, her expression softened, and she began to speak.

"I'm sorry. I was annoyed last night and I put you to sleep without asking. It was wrong of me and I shouldn't have done it. I'm very sorry and I won't do it again."

Rory was silent while he considered her apology.

"Okay," he said, finally. "Apology accepted."

"Regarding number two," she said. "I will try to make sure you know what I'm doing if I do something to you. But I will ask for special dispensation for certain situations when time presses. For example, if you were seriously injured, and I needed to take action quickly to save your life."

"I can accept that," Rory said. "As long as we both are in agreement about the principle."

"Finally, I promise that I will be honest and not lie to you. Although there are things I may not be able to tell you. Or that I may choose not to tell you, if I have good reasons."

"Good reasons," he repeated. "It smells like bullshit."

"I promise that I will only do it if I actually do have good reasons. And I promise that, if I ever do that, I will explain completely in the fullness of time. Good enough?"

Rory considered for a few moments and then nodded.

"Good enough. Thank you. I will be obedient now."

"Thank goodness."

"I wish we could just start this day over," Rory said. Before he had finished speaking, he found himself back in bed, still fully dressed, with Tseluna presenting a breast to him.

"Would you like some nummies?"

•　　　•　　　•

After lunch, Tseluna put a hand on Rory's shoulder and he felt the shift of teleportation. They arrived and Rory first felt a wave of truly oppressive heat followed by a constant grumbling roar. The ground shook under his feet. A fey red light colored everything and when he looked around he saw they were standing at the edge of a cinder cone of an erupting volcano with streams of lava running nearby. When he breathed in, he was nearly overpowered by the smell of brimstone.

"You'd better bring up your shield," Tseluna said. "And I want you to expand it so it covers me too."

"But I still can't do that!" Rory said.

"You don't want me to get hurt, do you?" she said. "In a few minutes, we'll have another shower of burning ash. Maybe even splashes of lava. If you don't cover me, I might get seriously injured."

"Can't you use your own shield?" he asked anxiously.

"I'm depending on you, Sugar," she said. "You can protect me, can't you?"

Rory brought up his shield and tried to make it expand, as he'd tried repeatedly before but without success. He could hear the volcano grumbling in the background. A sprinkling of ash fell on them.

"Ow! Ow! Ow!" squeaked Tseluna. "It hurts!"

"I'm trying!" Rory said desperately. He wracked his brain trying to think of anything he hadn't tried yet. He tried to visualize the shield separating from his body and moving out. But it stubbornly wouldn't move. He tried to imagine it swelling, blowing up like a balloon. He drew air into his lungs and puffed out his cheeks. And then he felt it.

"Help, Rory! It's erupting!" Tseluna whimpered. "I don't want to get burned! Help me!"

Rory tried to draw more air into his lungs, but his lungs were already full, but as he imagined swelling up more and more, he felt his shield ratcheting out, just an inch and then two. He tried to capture that feeling and push it farther.

The volcano spewed a huge discharge of ash that began to fall on them. Tseluna screamed. Rory closed his eyes and pushed as hard as he could. He felt the ash and larger scalding rocks falling on the shield. Then he felt Tseluna's arms around him. He opened his eyes and found that they were sharing the glowing bubble of his shield. He looked down into Tseluna's eyes and she grinned at him.

"I knew you could do it, Sugar," she said. "You just needed the right incentive. Next, you need to be able to create two shields: one around yourself and one that you can place around something else. But you can work on that later. For now, I think you deserve a reward."

She kissed him gently, pressing her rough tongue against his. He kissed her back passionately.

14

A FAMILY EVENT

(45 TRALONGS)

AS RORY GOT READY TO LEAVE for his training run one Wednesday morning, Tseluna teleported herself outside and rang the doorbell, as usual, but Rory's dad got to the door first.

"Good morning, Mrs. T," he said, opening the door. "Do you have a second?"

For a moment, Rory was filled with hope that they could skip the run.

"Certainly," she said, then turning to Rory. "You go ahead on your run." She patted him and pretended she was unaware of the stream of curses running through his mind.

During his whole run, he wondered what they could be talking about. He was on the last leg before the cool down when she suddenly zapped him from behind.

"Yow!" he said, putting on a burst of speed. She dogged him, making him run for all he was worth until they reached the last turn.

"Your father is trying to schedule your mother's family's reunion," Tseluna said casually, as Rory panted desperately trying to catch his breath. "He wanted to consult with me so as to minimize the impact on your training."

"Do I have to go? Can't you help me wriggle out?"

"He made a persuasive case that your mother's relatives would be very disappointed if you didn't attend. I said you could attend provided allowances were made for you to continue your training."

Rory made a rude noise.

"I did say you could skip running." Rory brightened. "Because you can start with an early-morning swim across the lake instead." Rory's hopes were dashed and Tseluna grinned tousling his hair.

"You leave tomorrow," she said. "Your father is getting your tickets today."

"Do I really need a ticket?"

"Well, no," she said. "But if we revealed you didn't need one, it might shed light on the deception we are practicing."

"And we couldn't have that," Rory said.

"No, we couldn't," Tseluna agreed with a laugh. "And anyone who revealed that would probably need to be severely punished."

"I'll make sure I get my ticket," Rory said carefully.

•　　　•　　　•

Rory and Tseluna arrived at the Blink Station and checked in. After standing in line, Rory showed his ticket at the counter. The agent checked his documents, noted his suitcase, and checked the annotation for his familiar.

"You're all set, sir," she said. "Proceed through Gate 1 to Central Hub."

He started to walk toward Gate 1.

"Go into one of the bathrooms," Tseluna directed.

"Do you need to use the bathroom or something," Rory asked, puzzled.

"Not hardly," she retorted. "But you don't think you're going to get me to go into one of those Blink portals, do you?"

"What? I thought they were perfectly safe."

"Bah!"

Rory stepped into a stall and felt the now totally ordinary shift of teleportation. He opened the stall and found he was in a different bathroom.

"Where are we?"

"You'll see."

Rory left the bathroom and found he was near the exit of the Blink Station in Mapleton. He walked to the checkout. The attendant checked his ticket, looked at his watch and then listened to it.

"Wow!" he said, returning his ticket. "How did you get here so fast?"

"I ran all the way," Rory joked.

He walked out of the exit and saw his uncle Bill waiting by the door.

"Rory!" he called. Rory walked over and accepted a hug.

"And this is my ... familiar, Tseluna," Rory said.

"Hello, Tseluna. It's nice to meet you!" Bill said, rubbing Tseluna under her chin. "You're really beautiful, aren't you."

"Oh, I like him," Tseluna subvocalized to Rory, purring.

Bill stepped back and looked Rory up and down.

"You've grown a lot in the past—What has it been?—two years?" he said. "Thank you for coming. Grandma and Grandpa will be so happy to see you. And your cousins have been asking about you too."

Rory blushed, remembering how he'd tried to get out of coming. They started walking toward the lake house.

"How's your dad?" Bill asked, after a few moments of silence.

"He's okay, I guess," Rory said. "I don't see him that much, to be honest. But we make time to have dinner together nearly every night."

"It must be really hard for him too," Bill said. "How are your classes going? And what's this scholarship you got?"

"School is okay," Rory said. "A lot of it seems boring. The scholarship is cool. I'm learning defense magic and will compete in a tournament at the end of the summer."

"Your dad said he promised your coach that you'd keep training. Can you make yourself practice without your coach here?"

"Yes," Rory assured him. "There's no danger of me slacking off."

"I heard she's pretty fierce."

"That's one word for it."

"I also heard she's pretty attractive."

"I ... I guess so," Rory said, wishing he could change the subject.

They turned the last corner and Rory could see the lake house perched among big trees on the slope that led down to the large lake beyond. It looked much as it had in previous years and then Rory realized it was the first year he was visiting it without his mom. It was as though the sun went behind a cloud and he shivered for a moment.

"Are you alright?" Tseluna asked in his head, and it was like a ray of sunlight in his darkness. "It's okay. I'm here with you, Sugar."

"Thank you," he thought to her and felt the warmth of her regard.

Uncle Bill opened the door and held it for him.

"We've put all the boys in the basement," he said. "Tammy is sleeping with us in the guest room."

Rory took his suitcase downstairs and saw that the single bed had been set aside for him with the younger cousins using the bunk beds. He left his suitcase then returned upstairs where everyone was in the dining room having lunch. He introduced Tseluna then hugged his grandma and grandpa and Aunt Sally. The cousins waved at him, busily eating their sandwiches while he fixed his own with the bread, meat, cheese, and other fixings that had been set out on the sideboard.

After lunch, Grandma handed Rory and each of the cousins a 100 spess note. "Why don't you kids all go to the corner store and buy yourselves a little treat?" She looked at Rory. "Does your ... familiar need a treat?" Rory shook his head, after consulting with Tseluna.

Rory noticed that his cousins seemed apprehensive, but they accepted the money and headed out into the afternoon heat.

"I'm not sure I want to go to the store," Tammy said, once they were out of sight of the house. The boys nodded.

"Did something happen the last time you went?" Rory asked. They looked reluctant to talk.

"They ran into some bullies who threatened them and stole their money," Tseluna told him. As usual, she mind-probed first and asked questions later.

"Don't worry," Rory assured them. "It will be fine today."

They were reassured though still apprehensive as they approached the country store.

"Look who it is, Roy," said a lanky youth, who stepped out around the corner of the store. "It's those brats bringing us more beer money."

"Right you are, Lester," said a larger young man, coming up from behind them along with an even bigger man, who looked a bit simple and only grunted.

"Try to do this without magic," Tseluna subvocalized. "But don't let them hurt you either."

"Here," said Rory. He handed Tseluna to Tammy and turned to face the bullies.

"I recommend you back off," said Rory evenly, though his heart rate went way up as he perceived they were not going to give up without a fight.

The big dumb one charged him, and Rory calmly sidestepped, catching his arm in an hold, sending him sprawling onto the pavement, immobilized. Rory then made an abortive foot strike at the back of his neck, meeting the eyes of the other bullies, who immediately understood that Rory had passed up following through on a disabling blow.

At this point, Rory realized that, although he felt no closer to being able to put a hand on Tseluna, three hours of aikido practice a day for a month and a half had caused his skills to progress dramatically and ordinary people had no hope of putting a hand on him either.

The other two both charged at Rory from opposite directions, but ended up running into each other, when Rory simply slipped to the side. They fell, tangled up with each other.

"If you continue, you're going to get hurt," Rory said. "Walk away—if you want to still be able to walk."

"You've made your point, mister," one said.

"If you come around us again," Rory said quietly, making a fist and shaking it gently at them. "I will make certain that you're very, very sorry."

He returned to the cousins, who were standing with their mouths open. He accepted Tseluna back from Tammy, then opened the door for them.

"After you!"

Walking back, the cousins were ecstatic with Rory's performance and acted out different parts as they repeated what they could remember of the dialog.

"What is that? How do you do that?"

"It's called 'aikido'," Rory said. "It teaches you how to use an opponent's force against them."

"Can you teach me?" the oldest, Billy asked.

"I wanna learn too!" Mikey said.

"Me too!" Tammy said.

"What do you think?" Rory subvocalized to Tseluna.

"Well, you need to practice anyway ..." Tseluna said.

"Okay," Rory said. "When we get back, make sure it's okay with your mom and dad and I'll start to teach you. But don't expect miracles. It takes a long time and a lot of practice to get good."

When they returned, the cousins ran in and were all trying to tell the story of what happened at the same time. Rory went to the backyard, assumed *seiza* position and began to meditate.

Uncle Bill came out after a few minutes. "Are you okay?" he asked.

Rory grinned. "I'm fine," he said. "It was no big deal."

"It kinda sounds like it was a big deal," he said. "Do you think those boys will back off? Or are they likely to cause more trouble."

"More trouble," Tseluna said to Rory instantly.

"They will probably try to cause more trouble," Rory said to Bill. "But we will be prepared."

When the cousins came out, Rory explained aikido the way Tseluna had explained it to him. Next, he led them in meditation and then the first few forms of movement. Then they spent the rest of the afternoon swimming close to the dock and having fun.

That night, Tseluna woke Rory in the wee hours of the morning.

"They're here," she said. "They are planning to set the house on fire."

"Should I just kill them?" Rory asked.

"Well, aren't we bloodthirsty," Tseluna chided. "Why don't we try once more to persuade them to straighten up. I've got an idea."

"What should I do?"

"Why don't you take advantage of this opportunity to try putting them to sleep."

"What if I make a mistake?"

"Eh. No big deal," Tseluna said. "I mean, you were ready to kill them a minute ago anyway."

Rory got out of bed and snuck out the door from the basement to the back yard. Tseluna directed him toward where the three young men were approaching the house carrying a large jug.

"What's in the jug?" Rory asked.

"It's some kind of flammable solvent," she said. "I can't tell what it is from here and he doesn't know either, the idiot."

Rory tried to gather a tiny amount of power and then he reached out and carefully stroked the hypothalamus of the one furthest back, who conked out very satisfactorily. Rory did the next who also collapsed. It took two tries to get the last one, but he was just pleased he hadn't killed them.

"Okay," he said. "Now what?"

When he looked again, they were gone.

"Where did you send them?"

"Oh, it's a tiny island in the far north," she said. "There's nothing there but tundra with lichens and little willows."

"Won't they freeze?"

"It's not that cold at this time of year. Not usually. You should catch up on your sleep and then have breakfast. We can go have a little conversation with them later in the morning."

Rory and Tseluna returned to the lake house, crept in the back door, and got back into bed. Tseluna purred and rubbed her head on Rory as he went back to sleep.

The next morning, Rory woke up and smelled bacon. The cousins were already up and he could hear voices upstairs.

"Should we go check on the would-be arsonists?" he asked Tseluna.

"Why don't you have breakfast first," she said. "There's no rush."

"It does smell good," he admitted.

Rory trotted upstairs, carrying Tseluna on his shoulder, and went into the dining room where everyone greeted him warmly.

"Can I make you some eggs?" Grandma asked.

"Scrambled?"

"You've got it," she said, bustling into the kitchen.

Rory listened to Billy try to tell a joke and they all laughed even harder when he got the punchline wrong so then they all started trying to tell other jokes and get the punchlines wrong on purpose.

"Here you go, honey," Grandma said, handing him a plate with eggs, bacon, and toast.

"Do you want any?" he subvocalized to Tseluna.

"You know I don't have to eat."

"I know you don't have to, but would you like a piece of bacon?"

"Well, if you insist," she said and he could sense her smile which made him happy. He broke off a little piece of bacon and handed it to her on his shoulder.

"That's a pretty small kitten," Grandma said. "Is it okay to give her bacon?"

"It's fine, Grandma," he said.

"I knew there was a reason I didn't make you go swimming this morning," Tseluna purred.

"Oh, that's right!" he subvocalized back.

"Well, your sleep was disturbed," Tseluna continued. "Plus, it will be better during the hotter part of the day."

"I'll give you another piece of bacon, if we can skip the swim altogether," Rory teased.

"Don't push it, *Baka*."

After breakfast, Rory begged a few minutes to go for a little walk by himself and promised to come back promptly and teach aikido. He took Tseluna and they walked a short distance into the woods.

"Let's try 'good cop bad cop,'" Tseluna suggested.

"What does that mean?" Rory asked.

"It means that we will play roles with one of us being friendly while the other scares the crap out of them."

"Which role do I play? Good cop?"

"Well, I've had a lot of practice being terrifying," Tseluna said. "I think you should use this as a chance to try being scary. It's a good learning opportunity."

"What should I do?"

"Are you angry?"

"Yeah?"

"Well, show it! Didn't you want to kill them for what they did?"

"At the very least!" he said, starting to get into the spirit of things. "But I would want them to suffer first."

"Yeah? Well, let them know that. In fact, you can actually try to kill them," she said. "I'll hold you back. Probably."

"Yeah!" he growled, making a fist.

"Ready?"

"Ready!"

He felt the twist in his gut and they appeared on the shore of a chilly island under a foggy sky. The sun was a low red dot near the horizon. The three young men were huddled together on the shore a few yards away. Tseluna had transformed into her persona of Mrs. T, wearing a conservative suit with dark eyes.

"There you bastards are," Rory snarled at them. "I told you what was going to happen if I ever saw you again, but you couldn't take a hint."

"What did you do to us? Where are we?" the lanky one, maybe Lester, said. "This is abduction and kidnapping. They send you to prison for shit like this."

"I think you mean 'murder,'" Rory hissed. "But only if they find the bodies." The young men leapt to their feet.

"You wouldn't dare!"

"Now, now," Tseluna said. "I'm sure these young men will see reason ..."

"No way! I'm going to prosecute!" Roy said. "You can't treat people like this. My dad's a constable and I'm going make sure you get arrested and sent to prison."

"I don't think you appreciate ..." Tseluna started to say.

"No! You don't!" Lester said. "You're going down, you psycho freaks!"

"Let me kill them!" Rory pleaded.

"You can have them," Tseluna said, turning her back.

Rory rubbed his hands and a big grin broke out over his face.

"I think I'll cut their hands off first. And then their feet."

"Wait! Let's just boil them!" Tseluna said. She gestured and there was a giant cauldron, ten feet across, full of water over a fire on the beach.

"Where did you find that cool pot?" Rory asked, genuinely curious.

"Do you like that?" she said, pleased. "I saw it at those ruins where we were practicing the other day and thought it might come in handy."

"What are you talking about? Are you serious?" Roy said.

"Shut up," Rory snarled. "Once the water starts to boil, we'll throw you in and see how long you can tread water."

"Why wait?" Tseluna said. She gestured and invisible forces threw all three young men into the cauldron. They started screaming and thrashing around in the pot of lukewarm water.

"Wait. I thought you were supposed to be the good cop," Rory asked.

"Why bother," Tseluna said, as they dragged themselves out.

"Wait, wait, wait!" pleaded the biggest one, who'd said nothing up until now. "I'm sorry! Okay? I'm really sorry. I won't ever do anything bad ever again. Please don't kill me!"

Rory and Tseluna looked at each other and shook their heads sadly.

Roy and Lester joined in the chorus.

"We're sorry too. Please don't kill us. We won't say anything. We won't bother you again! We promise!"

"Well," Tseluna said after a long moment. "Maybe we can let them off this time."

"I don't know. Don't you think they need something to remind them?" Rory said, baring his teeth and holding up a pinky. "Maybe a finger? Or an ear?"

"Well, let's try this," Tseluna said. "We can always find them, if we really want."

Then she gestured and they vanished. Then she turned to Rory, and embraced him.

"Well done! You were really scary," she said, pulling him close and moving to kiss him. "I think you deserve a reward for that performance."

But Rory just stood there, looking down.

"What's wrong?"

"Can you change your appearance?" Rory mumbled. "It feels weird to do it with Mrs. T."

He looked again and Tseluna had reverted to her usual appearance, naked with her bright yellow eyes. Rory put his arms around her and they kissed for a long, long time.

"Don't forget your aikido lessons. And you still have to swim across the lake," she said.

●　　　●　　　●

Rory changed into his swimming trunks and then walked down to the dock. The sun was near its zenith and the heat of the day was becoming oppressive.

"Are you really going to swim all the way across?" Tammy asked, her eyes wide.

"Yep," Rory said. "And all the way back."

"What if you get tired?" Michael asked. Rory couldn't tell him that Tseluna could teleport him, so he just tousled his hair and then walked briskly out to the end of the dock and dove into the water. It was cold, but it felt good on the hot day.

Rory started swimming. He quickly fell into a comfortable rhythm swimming freestyle. Swimming gave him lots of time to think, so he let his mind wander. For all he complained about the long runs, and now the long swim, he rather liked it. As long he was engaged, he didn't have to worry about other demands being made on him. Unless Tseluna decided to zap him for not swimming fast enough. But he couldn't imagine she would do that. Would she?

He was now far out in the lake. He kept swimming easily, two strokes to each breath. He noticed a sailboat bearing down on him. He treaded water for a minute when they hailed him. He noticed, with his low body-fat, that if he stopped treading water, he would sink like a stone.

"You're pretty far out. Are you okay?"

There were two men drinking beer and two girls farther back in the boat.

"I'm fine. Thank you," Rory said and started swimming again.

As the sailboat went past, he heard the girls comment, "Did you see his muscles? What a hottie!" And he grinned as he kept swimming.

When he reached the three-quarters point, he rolled over on his back and took a break, just lazily kicking along and looking up at the brilliant blue sky with a few puffy, white clouds. After a couple of minutes, he rolled back over and returned to his comfortable stroke.

He didn't realize he'd reached the other side until he started bumping the bottom with his feet. He turned, got his feet under him, and stood. He looked back where he could see everyone clustered along the shore watching him. He raised his arms over his head and the cousins, standing on the dock, began jumping up and down.

He looked around for a minute, having swum all the way over. This section of coastline was undeveloped with trees down to the shore.

"Better start back," Tseluna told him. "Before you start to stiffen up."

Rory sighed and started the long swim back.

•   •   •

While it was still cool the next morning, Rory was practicing aikido forms in the backyard when his grandfather came down.

"Can I get your help with something?" he asked.

"Sure, Grandpa," Rory said. He followed his grandfather out to the shed.

"Can you grab my toolbox and bring it with you?"

"Okay," Rory said, picking it up and carrying it, as he followed his grandfather down to the dock.

"Yesterday, I saw that some of these nails had popped," he said. "And I wanted to drive them back down before someone gets hurt."

"I can do that, Grandpa," Rory said. He got out a hammer.

"Grab that nail setter too," Grandpa directed. Rory dug around in the toolbox until he found it. Grandpa walked along and pointed out nails that were just beginning to protrude above the wood. Rory went along on his hands and knees and drove them back down.

By the time they were finished, the day had become hot and Rory's grandfather was sweating.

"Let's get you out of the sun, Grandpa," Rory said. He picked up the tool box and started to carry it back to the shed. Then he heard a groan and saw his grandfather clutch at his chest.

"Grandpa!" Rory shouted and dropped the toolbox. He caught his grandfather and helped him lay down on the dock. "Are you okay?"

"His heart is fibrillating," Tseluna told him. "I'm going to borrow your body to try to get his heart restarted."

Suddenly, Rory was a passive observer while his body sprang into action. He quickly tore open his grandfather's shirt, brought up his shield, and placed his hands on his grandfather's chest. He felt Tseluna trigger an electrical charge between his hands. His grandfather jerked. She put his hand on his grandfather's chest assessing his heartbeat, then she shocked him again.

"Okay," she said, finally. "His heart is beating normally again. But he should still visit a medical facility."

Rory found he was in control of his body once more. Uncle Bill, having heard Rory's shout, came running down.

"Is it his heart?"

"I'm alright," Grandpa said, weakly. "Thanks to Rory."

"Just rest there, Pop. The doctor is coming."

Rory stayed with his grandfather and held his hand until the doctor and several orderlies arrived. They picked him up with a stretcher and carried him back to the local clinic.

Once his grandfather was gone and there was nothing more to do, Rory was overwhelmed by his emotions and found he had to go into the bathroom to cry. He sat on the toilet for several minutes sobbing, trying to keep quiet, and hoping that people wouldn't hear him. Then he felt arms enclosing him, Tseluna kissed him on top of his head, and gently rocked him back and forth.

"Ssh. Ssh. It's okay. You're a good boy. You did very well."

He put his arms around her and wept while she held him.

That night, after dinner, Rory was helping his grandmother clean up. She washed the dishes and he dried them and put them away. After they were done, his grandmother asked, "Do you have a minute, honey?"

"Sure, Grandma," Rory said, picking up Tseluna. She led him into her sitting room, shut the door, invited him to sit, then picked up her knitting and began to knit.

"May I speak with your familiar?" she said.

"What? Of course, Grandma," Rory said, mystified.

"I wasn't talking to you, honey," she said.

"He may speak freely," Tseluna said. Rory looked with shock to the side, to see Tseluna sitting next to him in human form.

"Thank you," Grandma said. Then she looked seriously at Rory.

"Are you happy with how things are?" she said. "Is this what you want?"

Rory was floored and it took him several moments to marshal his thoughts and reply.

"Yes, Grandma," Rory said. "I'm very happy. It's everything I've ever dreamed of and more."

"It was a big surprise to me when I saw you show up with a demon," she said, peering at Tseluna. "We don't see demons very often here."

"You've seen demons before?" Rory asked.

"During the war," she said. "I was in Operations. The other side had a man bound to a demon. Like you are. We caught the man and tried to separate him from the demon, but the demon killed him before it escaped."

She looked at Tseluna.

"Was that you?"

"It was not," Tseluna said.

"It was you who saved my husband's life, though, wasn't it?" Tseluna nodded.

"Thank you," Grandma Maetin said. Then her expression, which had marginally softened, grew deadly serious.

"But you must understand," she continued. "This is my precious grandson. I won't tell you to release him because he doesn't want that. Although I'm sure I don't need to say it, I will anyway: I will be ... disappointed if you do not take very good care of him."

"Your concern is noted," Tseluna said, putting an arm around Rory. "This one has great potential and I will do whatever it takes to bring him to the very peak of his abilities."

"Is she working you hard? Keeping you busy?" Grandma asked Rory.

"Yes, Grandma," Rory said. "She makes me get up early, eat right, train hard, and get enough sleep."

"Well, that's good then. I'm satisfied," she said. "Thank you both, Tseluna and Rory, for satisfying an old woman's curiosity."

•　　　•　　　•

At the end of the week, Uncle Bill walked Rory, with Tseluna perched on his shoulder, back to the Blink Station for his trip home. Rory was glad he'd come and felt guilty for having tried to get out of the trip.

"Thank you again for coming. Your cousins were really happy to see you again," Bill said. "All of us were. And thank goodness you were there for Grandpa!"

"I was nervous about coming," Rory said. "But I'm glad I did. I'm glad he's doing better."

"Will your coach be satisfied with how much training you were able to accomplish while you were here?"

"I think so," Rory grinned. "It's almost like I can hear her now."

15

UNFAMILIAR PRACTICE
(35 TRALONGS)

RORY AND TSELUNA were in the last stretch of the morning run, walking to cool down during the final quarter mile. He had guilted her into running with him again. Ahead, standing in the middle of the road, was a man wearing an outlandish robe and hat.

"What's his deal?" Rory asked.

"I think he's getting ready to attack you," Tseluna said, studying his magical energies.

Sure enough, a moment later, he waved his arms and sent a magic missile toward Rory. Rory casually raised his shield and the missile ricocheted off. He continued walking at a leisurely pace with Tseluna.

The man waved his arms again and sent another and another. And they also glanced off.

"This is getting tedious," Rory said, rolling his eyes.

"Hey! Hey!" he yelled at the guy. "Can you cut it out? That's annoying!"

The guy got really angry and, waving his arms, sent another barrage of magic missiles that all skipped off Rory's shield flying one way and another.

"*Baka!*" Tseluna said. "One almost hit me!"

"Hey!" Rory yelled at the guy. "If you hit my ... uh ... my coach, I'm going to be really angry."

"Rory!" she said. "Put a second shield around me."

In response, the guy sent a barrage of missiles directly at Tseluna. Rory quickly extended his shield so it covered her too and again the missiles just bounced and scattered. She slapped his head.

"Ow!" he said.

"Hey! I want my own shield," she said.

"But ..."

"Try!"

Rory closed his eyes and tried to visualize what he wanted, then he silently triggered another shield while keeping up the first. He cautiously opened his eyes and looked. Now Tseluna was enclosed in a separate shield. Rory tried to relax the size of his original shield and had this odd sensation, rather like when switching his attention from one eye to the other. For a moment, he almost lost control of the shields. But then he recovered and gained confidence with how to control them separately.

Another swarm of magic missiles came down the street and bounced harmlessly away.

"This guy is really pissing me *off*," Rory said. Now only about 20 feet away, he suddenly sprinted, as the guy sent one final barrage of missiles that had no more effect than the previous ones. Distracted by casting the spell, the guy realized how close Rory was, but it was too late, Rory punched him in the face and laid him out on the ground.

"Who are you? Why are you attacking us?" Rory shouted, but the guy was unconscious and couldn't answer.

"He was hired by the same thug that was trying to extort the jewelry store," Tseluna said, catching up. "The same guy who sent the goons to attack you on the bridge."

Rory drew back his leg to kick him, but Tseluna said, "That's enough. Good boy! Come inside and I'll give you your reward." He blushed as she took his arm and let him escort her into the house.

On the way in, Rory collected the mail and, among the usual bills, found a postcard addressed to him. It was an invitation to a class party down by the river for Tuesday.

"It's too bad we're so busy," he said, tossing it in the trash.

"We're not that busy," said Tseluna. "But nice try."

"What?"

"You're just saying that you're too busy because you don't want to go. But maybe I want to go! And I'll work you extra hard the next two days so you have the time!"

Rory rolled his eyes and pulled the card back out of the trash. Tseluna, who had proactively dropped her Mrs. T persona, caught him up in her arms.

"Now, let me give you your reward ..." she said, looking up into his eyes and twirling a lock of his hair around her finger. He slipped his arms around her and pulled her to him.

•   •   •

The next morning, Rory was awakened by the crash of thunder. He snuggled back under the covers, eyes closed, expecting a delay, if not outright cancellation, of the morning run.

"Don't get too comfortable," Tseluna said, slipping into bed with him.

"But there's thunder and lightning!" Rory said. "It's not safe!"

"What? Are you three years old?"

"What! It's lightning!"

"Don't you have a shield?"

"But ... I ... It's wet! I might slip and fall!"

"That's the most pathetic excuse I've ever heard," she said. "I should zap you just for thinking it, let alone saying it out loud. But, if the rain really is a problem ..."

She looked at Rory who opened his eyes cautiously and nodded.

"Let me take you someplace where it's not raining."

After she nursed him, he got dressed and put on his shoes. While he was still tying his shoes, she opened a portal and offered him a hand. He looked up and through to a harsh landscape of rocks and dirt with rugged mountains in the background.

"Is this Japan?" he asked.

"It's nearby. It's called Death Valley. C'mon!"

He took her hand and stepped through. The first thing he noticed was the heat. It was swelteringly hot. It was unbelievably hot. He literally couldn't believe someplace could be so hot.

"It's too hot!" he said. "I'm going to die."

"Aw, poor baby. But it's not raining! It hasn't rained here for years. You're just so full of complaints this morning! As long as you've brought plenty of water, you'll be fine."

"But I didn't bring any water," Rory said, beginning to feel put upon. "You didn't tell me I needed to bring any!"

"I can give you water, Sugar," she said, chuckling. "You'll feel better once you start running."

He looked at her suspiciously, but her grin was infectious and soon he was smiling too. He started walking and, after a few minutes, broke into an easy jog.

They ran along the margin of a wide flat, black surface with lines painted on it. On one side, there were vast, fan-shaped hills that rose to rugged mountains that were relatively nearby. The other side was a flat, blinding-white plain that stretched into the distance with mountains visible a long way off. There was literally no vegetation in view. Just dirt and rocks—and the white plain.

"What's the white stuff?" he asked.

"Oh. It's mostly salt," Tseluna said. "This place is way below sea level: any rain that falls here drains down to the salt flats and then evaporates, leaving the salt behind."

Rory ran for a while in silence. He was hot, it was true. But as soon as he sweated the sweat evaporated and it wasn't half as bad as he'd thought it would be.

"Here, Sugar," she said, handing him a cold bottle of water. "You do need to drink a lot when it's hot."

Rory took a few swallows and kept running. He heard an odd sound behind him and then suddenly there was a deafening howl. Rory brought up his shield and spun, collecting magical energy for a fireball. A gigantic metal and glass monstrosity was bearing down on him. It roared by in a cloud of dust. As it passed, he perceived that there was a person inside controlling it. He watched it pass and then looked back at Tseluna who was laughing so hard she looked in serious danger of passing out. He turned bright red and started running again.

"I'm sorry, Sugar," Tseluna said, after a minute of silence. "It was mean of me to laugh at you."

"No, I'm sure it was pretty funny," Rory said.

"Turn right here," Tseluna said, as they approached a trail that led out into the salt flats.

Rory did as she told him and they left the road behind. When he finished the first bottle of water, she handed him a fresh bottle that was also icy cold. He pressed the bottle against his temple before opening it.

"Where are you getting these bottles of water?" he asked. "They're so nice and refreshing!"

"It's a little embarrassing," she said.

"Why?"

"Well, there's a machine that sells water. And I get them from there."

"What's embarrassing about that?" he said. "But how do you buy them while you're here?"

"That's just it. I can't. So I just teleport them out of the machine without buying them."

"So, you're feeling guilty about stealing bottles of water?"

"Oh, no. I'm not stealing them. They're my bottles of water. I just feel guilty for the person that has to fill up the machine."

"They're your bottles of water?" he asked, scrunching up his face. "Is it your machine too?"

"Um. Yeah? I'll show it to you sometime."

They ran and ran, farther and farther out into the blinding salt-flats during the heat of the afternoon.

"You weren't kidding about working me hard," Rory said, beginning to approach his limit.

"You did well, though," Tseluna said. "It's nearly time for us to head back."

"Oh. Time dilation, right?"

"Yep. It's almost dinner time already," she said. She opened a portal and they stepped through into his bedroom. Rory opened the door to his bedroom and his dad looked at him, red from the sun, with salt crusted all over his skin and clothes.

"What have you been doing in there?" he asked. "I haven't seen you once all day."

"You wouldn't believe me if I told you," Rory said, scuttling into the bathroom and locking the door.

•   •   •

The next morning, when Tseluna woke him up, it was still raining, though no thunder. Rory reluctantly got up and pulled his clothes on to go running. While he was tying his shoes, he felt the shift of teleportation and, when he straightened up, he found himself in the middle of some kind of ancient, ruined stadium. They were surrounded by a wall with tiered seating that rose many levels up to the top. But in a number of places along the top, the stonework had failed. And there were trees and shrubs growing in spots among the seats.

"We didn't step through a portal, so we're in the same dimension, right? But where are we?"

"This place was called Lampira," she said. "It was a bustling trade center 500 years ago. But when they set up the first Blink networks, it became irrelevant and eventually it was abandoned."

"Why are we here?"

"I thought you should practice sparring with magic in a stadium to get ready for the tournament. It's sort of like this, although much larger."

She directed him to stand 20 yards away and they faced one another.

"Ready?" she called.

"Ready!" Rory said, raising his shield.

Tseluna cast three fireballs at Rory in rapid succession. Rory tuned his shield for fire, then silently cast a windblade where Tseluna was headed. She doubled back and cast force. Rory re-tuned his shield and fired again.

They spent a couple of hours doing 20-minute bouts, trading attacks. Between bouts, they sat in the shade.

"No bottles of water in this dimension, huh?" Rory asked.

"Not cold anyway," she said, handing him one.

He looked at her.

"Don't ask."

He opened the bottle and drank deeply. It was warm but refreshing.

When they started the next bout, Rory recognized he was starting to get tired. He raised his shield and re-tuned it when Tseluna cast a fireball. Then suddenly she charged him. Startled, he spoke the word of power to cast a magic missile at her and his shield dropped with the fireball just feet away. Frozen, in a state of shock, he watched his death fly at him but a breath away. Then something blocked his vision. Tseluna had teleported herself just in front of him. The fireball struck her and set her on fire. Rory screamed as she collapsed. She was covered with burns and dropped like a dead thing. He panicked and wrung his hands trying to think of something—anything—he could do.

"*Baka!*" he heard in his head as her body dematerialized and then she rematerialized, uninjured. She stood with her hands on her hips looking at him angrily.

Rory gulped.

"I'm so sorry," he said, looking down. "If you hadn't saved me, that would have been me."

"Bad boy!" she said. "How many times have I told you? If you can't control your shield, you're a dead duck."

"I know, I know," he said, miserably. "I'm trying to stop. But it's really hard to unlearn something like that!"

She gathered him into her arms and hugged him. "It's okay, Sugar. It didn't really hurt me," she said. "We've been at it for a long time. Let's go someplace quiet and take the rest of the day off." He hugged her back and didn't want to ever let go.

16

A FAMILIAR OUTING

(32 TRALONGS)

O N TUESDAY, THE SKIES WERE CLEAR and Rory put on his swimsuit, then put on shorts, shirt, and sandals. He topped it off with a straw hat and sunglasses. He packed lunch and took a towel.

Tseluna climbed up on his shoulder and they set off walking to the river.

Two blocks on, Buck appeared from a side street with his tabby familiar.

"Hey! Team Cat!" he called. He looked at Tseluna. "Wow. She hasn't grown much. Is she okay?"

"She's fine," Rory said. "She's ... just a small breed."

Rory felt Tseluna's irritation and began to sweat.

"You won't believe all the things Miri has learned!" Buck said. "She's an amazing familiar!"

Tseluna made a disparaging noise in Rory's head.

"I'll bet," Rory said, ignoring Tseluna. "I'm sure you're an amazing trainer for her."

"Oh, I don't know," Buck said, blushing. "But the most important thing is to always be positive. Punishment is almost always counterproductive. But sometimes you do have to send a message."

"So I've learned," said Rory, dryly.

"Right? Here watch this!" Buck said, pointing toward the top of a large tree. "Miri! Cut down that pine cone!" Miri looked up at the pine cone and hissed. A wind blade sheared it off, it fell, and Buck caught it.

"See! Isn't that amazing? Can your familiar do anything like that?"

Suddenly, Rory's mouth began speaking against his will, "Tseluna! Cut down that pine tree!" Tseluna made a tiny meow and a giant windblade cut down the whole tree a foot above the ground and it fell back into the forest with a resounding crash.

Buck stood there for ten or fifteen seconds, blinking, then turned and silently continued walking.

They walked on for another block and then several more students from the class appeared. They welcomed them and pressed on. At the next street, Aimee joined up. She greeted Rory warmly, but scowled suspiciously at Tseluna.

They reached the eastern edge of town where the ground dropped away toward the river far below. The sun sparkled on the water. The river here spread out wide into practically a lake above the rapids. They began the long descent down to the water where there was a small beach maintained by the town with a rope defining the safe swimming area.

"Last one in is a rotten egg," Buck yelled and started running for the water. Most of the class joined him. But Rory rolled his eyes and just kept walking. Aimee also stayed back.

"They're like children!" she said, with disgust.

Rory grinned and Aimee smiled to see him looking cheerful.

"Are things okay with you?" she asked carefully.

"Yes," Rory said. "Things are going well."

"That's good," she said. "I've been really worried about you."

"Thank you," he said. "You're a good friend. I haven't always remembered to tell you how much I value our friendship."

"But I think I know," she said, blushing as she remembered Rory risking everything to save her life and then pleading on her behalf with Tseluna.

They arrived at the bottom of the hill, and everyone was already in the water splashing around. Rory took off his shirt and shorts that he was wearing over his swim suit. Suddenly a whistle went up from someone. Rory realized everyone was looking at him.

"What?" he said.

"Your muscles ... They're huge! And it's like you can see every single one. Were you always like this? What have you been doing?" Buck asked.

"I dunno. Training?" Rory said.

"You should market your training routine," he said. "That's unbelievable. It even makes you look taller too."

Tseluna was almost insufferably smug.

Rory left Tseluna with his clothes and waded out into the water. Aimee was disgusted to see four or five girls surrounding Rory touching his muscles to "see what they felt like." She sat irritably up on the beach.

"You're lucky to be a cat so it doesn't make you jealous to have girls paying attention to him like that," she said grumpily to Tseluna.

Suddenly, the girls surrounding Rory all shrieked when they simultaneously experienced wardrobe malfunctions and their bathing suit tops fell off. They squealed, wrapped their arms around themselves, and came running up out of the water to put on shirts while they tried to figure out what had happened.

"Thank you!" Aimee whispered to Tseluna.

"Hey! Look!" Buck called. "Miri caught a fish!" He held up a tiny minnow that she'd pulled out of the river.

"Oh, no!" Rory thought, looking at Tseluna.

Tseluna went out onto the dock that extended twenty or thirty yards into the river.

"Don't do it!" Rory thought desperately.

Rory was looking right at Tseluna but still couldn't figure out how she did it. He just rolled his eyes and sighed.

"Hey! Look, everyone!" he called. "Tseluna caught a fish too!" Next to Tseluna, a huge catfish was flopping around on the dock. It was more than a yard in length and must have weighed a hundred pounds. Everyone stared and then started laughing as the fish finally flipped itself back into the water. Tseluna blinked innocently and then licked her paws. Poor Buck was speechless.

The classmates played and chatted in small groups for a couple of hours, then everyone came out of the water to have lunch. Rory sat on his towel and fed bits of meat to Tseluna from his sandwich and poured her some milk in the lid of his milk bottle.

He leaned back and looked up the long slope to the town. Suddenly he noticed something. He stood to look more closely. It was like the hillside was moving. It *was* moving, he realized! The heavy rains had destabilized the soil and the hillside was slumping and sliding directly toward them.

"Avalanche!" he yelled, pointing. Everyone turned and watched with horror as a wall of mud, rocks, and trees came racing toward them with increasing speed. There were screams as everyone looked around in a panic with no-where to run.

"To me! To me!" Rory screamed. "Quick! Quick! Quick!" Everyone ran toward him as the wall of debris sped down upon them. Tseluna climbed up on his shoulder. Rory gathered as much power as he possibly could.

"Closer! Press together!" he yelled.

"Miri!" wailed Buck. Miri was still back playing by the water when an invisible force snatched her up and tossed her to Buck who caught her and held her close.

Rory gathered a vast amount of magical power. He silently triggered his shield and extended it out so it covered everyone. It glowed with a brilliant light just as the wave of mud and debris washed over them. Rory poured everything he could into maintaining the shield against the force of the flow. He could feel each rock and tree that slammed into the shield, but he kept pumping power into it to keep it up. At one point, the mud overtopped the shield and they were thrown into darkness but for the lambent glow of the shield itself. As the mudflow slowed and ceased, the level dropped a bit and they could see daylight again above the shield.

"Get ready, everyone," he warned and took the shield down. The mud slumped down into the void that the shield had created. People at the edges were left up to their hips in sticky mud.

There was silence and then suddenly there were deafening cheers as everyone pressed forward and tried to hug Rory at once.

"How did you do that? That was unbelievable! You saved us! That was like a miracle!" voices said all at once.

"And thank you for saving Miri," Buck said, tearing up. "If I had let something happen to her, I never would have been able to forgive myself."

Rory, who had been utterly fixated on casting the shield, had no idea what he was talking about until Tseluna showed him.

"Oh," he said. "It was Tseluna that saved her. You should thank her."

"Thank you, Tseluna," Buck said, earnestly. "You're the greatest!"

"Good boy," Tseluna subvocalized to Rory and he felt a little jolt of pleasure. "I'll give you a better reward when we get home."

17

UNFAMILIAR ODDS

(25 TRALONGS)

RORY RAN THROUGH TOWN on his usual early morning run. Tseluna had stayed behind again this morning. Rory scoffed at her laziness as he ran because he knew it would tease her. He got back a sense of annoyed irritation and carefully shifted his thoughts to other topics.

"Good morning," Aimee said, coming alongside him as he jogged.

"Good morning," he replied automatically. "Wait! Do you run?"

"I thought I would run with you because I've seen that Tseluna doesn't always come with you and I thought maybe we could have a private word."

He considered her statement for a moment. Early on, Tseluna had been unwilling to concede divulging any information that might put her plans at risk. But now, with the time for training coming to an end anyway, she seemed less concerned. So, Rory swallowed, took a risk, and spoke directly.

"Understand that you can have no private words with me," Rory said. "Tseluna can hear everything I hear and can read my thoughts at all times. She can also speak using my mouth and so be aware that you cannot be certain if I am speaking or she is speaking through me."

"Like right now," Tseluna said with his mouth. Rory gestured at his own head. Aimee looked at him with dawning realization.

"That must be awful," she said, with horror. "How can you stand it?"

"Actually," Rory said. "It was really uncomfortable at first, but now it's not. It's hard to explain. But she can not only hear my thoughts, she also can access all of my memories. I have no secrets from her. I can have no secrets. And that's somehow liberating."

"I don't get it," Aimee said. "That sounds ... even worse."

"I can be myself and be totally honest. I have to be honest. It's true that I have no ability to dissemble. But I also have no need. I don't know how to explain it, but it's liberating to be so completely accepted."

"Blech," Aimee said, a bit queasy just thinking about it.

"She knows absolutely everything about me. While it's true that she could be cruel, she's not. She's not like that."

"But I can't know if that's really you speaking or her making you say those things. While you have no secrets from her, the rest of us can't be sure of anything you say."

Rory nodded. Aimee began to pant and stumble.

"Oh," Rory said. "I think we can take a break for a minute."

They stopped at a bench at the town green under the immense chestnut tree and Aimee panted to catch her breath.

"What is she having you train for?" Aimee asked.

Rory consulted Tseluna and replied, "I'm not allowed to tell you that."

"How did you get so powerful?"

"I'm not allowed to talk about that either."

"Is she doing anything weird to you?"

"Define 'weird' ..."

"You know ... like ... sex things."

"I will decline to answer that on the grounds that I might incriminate myself," Rory said, his ears coloring.

"Is she having sex with you?"

"Nothing so ... normal," he admitted. Then he stood. "Tseluna tells me I need to start running again."

"You're going to be okay, aren't you?" Aimee asked, perhaps more desperately than she intended.

"I don't know," Rory said. "But I will say that I wouldn't trade it for the world."

Aimee came to her feet and threw herself against him. He stood for a moment while she hugged him, and then enfolded her in his arms and hugged her back.

"Please be safe," she whispered.

"Thank you," he said. Then he pulled away and started to run again.

•　　　•　　　•

"Soon, I'm planning to take you to my home dimension," Tseluna said.

"Are you going to introduce me to your parents?" Rory asked with a grin.

"Well, two things. First, demons would not think of you as a someone to 'meet.' So I will be showing you, not introducing you," she said. "But not to my parents because demons do not have parents. Demons arise spontaneously from the high concentration of magic. Most die or are killed very quickly. But a few survive and become strong enough to reach what you might consider adulthood."

"How creepy," Rory thought. Then remembered Tseluna could read his mind and flushed with embarrassment. But Tseluna made no comment.

"Wait ..." Rory said, as something occurred to him. "Aren't baby demons sort of like elementals then?"

"That's exactly right," Tseluna said. "In a high-magic dimension, an elemental could continue to develop, potentially becoming a demon. But there's not enough magic here for that to happen.

"At the moment, however, what I would like to teach you is how to visualize flows of magic," she said. "Demons often barely notice what you might think of as the physical world. So when we're in the demon dimension, you won't be able to appreciate the environment if you can't see the magic.

"The 'right' way to do this is to create a layer of magic inside your eye that is sensitive to magic and can make it show up in your vision. But if you're not careful—or you lack finesse—you can easily damage your eyes that way."

She looked at Rory and he said, "Is the 'wrong' way safer?"

"Yes, exactly. Do you have any sunglasses?"

Rory stepped across the room and went through the top drawer of his dresser until he found the sunglasses he'd put away after going to the river earlier.

"Will these do?"

"Yes, perfect. Let me show you this way ..."

Suddenly, Rory saw a complex magical symbol in his mind's eye.

"What? You can show me things in my head?"

"This is what you need to do in each eye of the glasses. Give it a try."

Rory studied the symbol and marshaled some magic power. He was about to speak a word of power when he heard Tseluna draw her breath in, and he instead initiated the spell silently. She let her breath out. Then he held the glasses up to his face.

"Whoa."

He looked at his hand first, which had complex flows of magic through it. He could also see the cord running from his collar to Tseluna and observe the flow of magic coming from her to him. Her magical energies did not actually look like her body at all. It was more like a swirling cloud of multicolored energies, with a brilliant core of lucent white.

"No wonder Aimee was suspicious," Rory said.

"Oh, no," Tseluna said, and suddenly her magical appearance transformed. The cloud was gone and she looked like a person with similar magical pathways to his own. "I can conceal my magical appearance when necessary, but I wanted you to see what demons actually look like, since that's where we'll be going."

"Okay," he said. "Anything else I should know?"

"I expect afterwards there will be things you wish you knew, but I think it's actually better you just go without preconceptions. You trust me, do you not?"

He looked at her, trying to imagine how he could express the depth of his trust and his love for Tseluna. She smiled to acknowledge that she perceived his earnest struggle and patted his head.

"Good boy! Go to sleep now. We'll go first thing tomorrow morning when you're fully rested."

In the morning, Tseluna woke Rory in the usual way. Afterward, rather than running, she simply directed him to get dressed and bring his sunglasses. Tseluna gestured and a portal opened. Beyond, Rory could only see swirling colors. Tseluna offered him a hand and he took a deep breath and stepped through.

He found himself floating in space. He panicked when he realized he couldn't tell which direction was up and he couldn't see anything but a smear of shifting vibrant colors.

"Put your glasses on!" Tseluna subvocalized. He slipped the sunglasses on and suddenly he was floating underwater with colorful fish swimming past. He panicked feeling like he was drowning.

"It's okay. Just breathe normally," Tseluna told him.

"Do we have to swim somewhere?" Rory asked.

"No. Here you simply move yourself using magic."

She pulled him along with her as they moved through a series of environments. After the fish, they were in a beautiful cave with glittering crystals. And then in a series of waterfalls.

"These are amazing," Rory said. "I've never even imagined such beautiful places."

"The demon that does these is a famous artist," Tseluna said. "They find the most beautiful places across the multiverse to create these experiences."

After passing through another mindblowing series of environments: the rings around a planet, the inside of an egg with a developing dragon embryo, just above the event horizon of a black hole ... Rory had no idea what he was seeing so Tseluna explained what some of the things were. Rory was floored.

"I had no idea that the universe was so ... big," he said, wonderingly, which made Tseluna laugh at his naivete.

They eventually flew toward what looked like a broad plaza. There was a kind of plinth that Tseluna set Rory upon. She made his collar visible, holding the cord in her hand.

"Here is my entrant in the Familiar Tournament," she announced.

Rory stood on the plinth and watched as first a few, then hundreds and then thousands of demons arrived. And then it started. He felt like he was being split or torn into pieces and all of a sudden it was like he was holding a dozen, a hundred, a thousand conversations all at once.

"Who are you? What are you? Where are you from? What can you do?"

He began to feel like he was going insane and started to collapse when Tseluna caught him and held him up.

"Demons are making copies of you to query in order to decide how much to wager on you," she said. "The worst is over. It will just be another two or three hours."

He could feel himself being asked many other personal questions and then directed to perform various spells. He heard himself answering honestly and earnestly which made him embarrassed, like he was a dog at a dog show. But it was just getting started.

Pain erupted all over his body as the demons began destructively testing their copies of him to see how much it would take to kill him. He would have collapsed but for Tseluna holding him up. She held him in her arms.

"It's not really happening," she whispered in his ear over and over. "It's okay. I've got you. You're okay."

He broke down in sobs and clung to her as he was killed in a thousand painful and creative fashions. He felt himself cut, smashed, crushed, burned, and destroyed in novel ways. It went on and on and on. After what seemed like an eternity, it finally came to an end.

Shuddering, he took one breath after another as he managed to get his feet back under him and stand on his own power.

"Look at that!" Tseluna crowed. "You got even odds!"

Rory tried to appreciate this fact. Trembling, he leaned on Tseluna before he collapsed again.

"Is that good?" he asked, wiping his eyes.

"Oh, yeah," Tseluna said, excited. "The best I ever got before was 1 in 3."

"What did that guy get last year?"

"Him? Oh. Um. 1 in 50? 1 in 100? Something like that. It wasn't good."

Rory tried to take pleasure from Tseluna's happiness, but he felt sick and shaky, like he might faint at any moment.

"Can we go home now?" he asked.

"Yes, yes," Tseluna said. Rory felt her reward him with a huge wave of pleasure, but it didn't even begin to touch his misery. "Let's get you home. You deserve a big reward tonight."

Rory let Tseluna put an arm under his shoulders to help hold him up. She opened a portal and helped him step through into his bedroom, where he collapsed into his bed. He pulled a pillow over his head sobbing. She climbed into bed with him and pulled him against her chest.

"Is this what you didn't tell me?" he whispered.

"Yeah," she said. "I knew it would be rough for you and thought it would be better if you didn't have to spend the whole night worrying about it."

"Thank you," he said. "If I'd known it would be that bad, I'm not sure I could have done it."

"You did very well," she said, holding him close. "Good boy!"

She gently stroked and patted him. Then she lifted his head up and kissed him very gently on the lips. He held on to her and quietly cried himself to sleep.

18

AN UNFAMILIAR TASK

(12 TRALONGS)

RORY AND TSELUNA WERE OUT for his usual daily run. As usual, she was about 10 paces back. They'd turned the far corner and were nearly halfway home when he ran through something. Upon reflection, it felt kind of like a spiderweb, but it was almost as though the air itself was thick or sticky. At the time, he didn't think too much about it until he felt his connection with Tseluna severed. He spun and looked back.

It looked to him like Tseluna was enclosed in a shimmering cylinder of glowing energy. It was like she was trapped in a jar of viscous liquid, like honey or oil. She seemed frozen, in some kind of stasis.

Rory panicked for a moment when he felt for her reassuring contact and was unable to reach her. He also did not have access to Tseluna's magical energy, which left him few options.

He decided that the device must be a trap laid by the demon that had been hunting Tseluna and that it would probably return soon. He resolved to study the device to see if he could figure out how it worked and how to break it.

He scrutinized the cylinder and, looking up, saw nothing, so he looked down at the ground. He knelt by the edge. He could see signs that the ground had been disturbed and swept. With his fingernail, he scratched at the dirt by the cylinder and found that a groove or trench had been inscribed in the surface of the path and filled with … salt? He tasted his finger and confirmed that it was salt. He could feel the spell inside, which was much more complicated. But it was enclosed and held together by a simple salt-circle barrier. That gave him an idea.

Rory looked around and saw the back of a house through the trees 100 yards away. He ran to the house and banged on the door. When a woman answered the door, he asked, "Please! Do you have a package of salt I could borrow?"

"Do you just want a shaker?"

"No, I need more than that," he said. "Do you have anything bigger?"

She returned from the kitchen and handed him a package of salt that was nearly full.

"Thanks, Ma'am!" Rory said and sprinted back.

He looked around carefully to confirm that the demon had not yet returned. Then he took a stick and made a very large circle that enclosed the entire device. He carefully left a line of salt inside, then covered his circle over, except for one tiny spot. Then he assumed *seiza* position and began to meditate as Tseluna had taught him to maintain awareness of his surroundings.

Forty minutes later, he felt a tickle on the back of his neck and realized the demon must be close. He had a powerful adrenaline rush, and his heart began to pound, but he forced himself to stay calm and give no overt reaction. He waited with no shield for the demon to show themself.

They materialized inside Rory's circle. He stabbed his finger down on the salt circle and invested it with as much energy as he could. Then he raised his shield and sprang toward the circle enclosing Tseluna. The demon hit Rory with some kind of magic missile that struck where he'd been sitting. It sliced through his shirt and left a long, shallow laceration across his shoulders and back. But then Rory ran his finger through the circle enclosing Tseluna and he felt the spell fall apart. He felt his connection to Tseluna restored. His shield roared to full strength just as the demon sent another magic missile. This one was barely deflected and stabbed deep into the ground by his ribs.

When the demon realized that Tseluna had been freed, they tried to escape, but discovered they were enclosed by Rory's circle. Before they could break the circle, Tseluna had them by the throat. He heard them exchange statements in their demon tongue, then Tseluna did something that produced a bright flash, and the other demon was gone.

"Finally!" Tseluna said. "That takes care of that guy."

She turned and looked at Rory.

"You know you could have let that demon take me and then you'd have been free of me," Tseluna said.

"But I don't want to be free of you," Rory mumbled. "Because I love you."

"What was that?" she said.

"I said you need to be more careful!" he said, knowing full well that she didn't need to hear him to know what he was thinking.

"What I think I need is to make sure to train you enough so that you survive the tournament," she said, approaching. "But you did well, Rory. You did very well indeed. Here is a reward." She held his face and kissed him forcefully, pushing her rough tongue inside his mouth. He hugged her as the adrenaline rush ended, leaving him shaky and weak.

"Let's just walk home," he said. "After I return this package of salt."

They walked in silence for some minutes and finally Rory could resist no longer.

"So ... Are you ever going to tell me who that demon is and why they keep attacking you?"

Tseluna glanced over at him and sighed.

"It's not really very interesting," she said. "But let me at least give you some context. First, let me ask you this: What's the arc, or trajectory, of a person's life?"

"Uh ..." Rory said, caught off guard by the change in subject. "Go to school. Get a job. Get married. Have kids. Retire. Die?"

"So what would you do if there is no school, you don't get married or have kids, and you don't die?"

"Get a job and retire?"

"And you've already done that."

"Uh ..."

"Exactly. This is the question that demons are confronted with. And different demons find different solutions—different ways to pass the time. I joined the D-Force for a while but there were a lot of politics involved and eventually I decided it was all bullshit so I quit. Then I had to decide what to do. I decided to explore low magic dimensions—in part because few demons ever do.

"Partly I was just avoiding other demons: I had made a lot of enemies. And partly I was just looking for something to do."

"And what does that have to do with this other demon?"

"Well, this other demon, like me, is looking for something to do. But their project seems to be making my life difficult."

"Are they angry at you because of what you did on the D-Force? Or politics?"

"I don't think so," she said. "They didn't start until more recently."

"Is it something to do with the tournament? Is this demon the relative of some other demon that was an enemy?"

"Demons don't have relatives, remember?"

"Augh," Rory said, putting his head in his hands. "That's right. What puzzles me is that the attacks don't seem very dangerous. I mean, the direwolves couldn't have really hurt you, right? And, this trap ... Couldn't they have made a trap that caused real damage rather than just immobilizing you?"

"That's true," Tseluna said, thoughtfully.

"And if the demon had wanted to hurt me, they could have at any number of points. But the attacks have been more of a nuisance than anything. Do you think maybe they're more of a fan than an enemy? Could they be looking for you to acknowledge them?"

"Acknowledge them?"

"Yeah," Rory said, warming to his theory. "Young people sometimes get frustrated when someone they have a crush on or admire seems like they're ignoring or disrespecting them. And they'll sometimes play practical jokes on someone to try to get them to acknowledge them. Sometimes these can escalate to dangerous levels. Could it be something like that?"

"Hmm. It could be, I guess."

"I can't understand what you're saying when you talk to them. Could it be you've not been taking them seriously? Maybe next time, you shouldn't dismiss them, but go all out. Give them what they're looking for."

"I'll keep that in mind."

•   •   •

In the afternoon, Tseluna teleported them to a remote valley Rory hadn't seen before. They were near the foot of a small bluff, 50 or 60 feet high, in a region of grassland with rolling hills.

"This afternoon, I want you to practice a specific skill," Tseluna said. "I've tried to impress on you that it's often not about raw power, but about using just enough power to do what you need."

"Is this going to be about dick-measuring contests again?" Rory said, rolling his eyes.

Tseluna smiled in a mean kind of way.

"Sort of like that. I want you to stand here. I'm going to go up there," she said, gesturing to the top of the bluff. "I'm going to throw things at you and, without moving, I want you to avoid getting hit. I'll start with small ones, but then they'll get bigger."

"Small what?" Rory said, apprehensively.

"You'll see," Tseluna said with a wink. She teleported up to the top of the cliff.

"Ready?" she subvocalized.

"Ready!" he yelled.

She gestured and ... something dark and round appeared over the lip of the cliff and accelerated toward him as it fell. He activated his shield and then reached out his hand and exerted force on the whatever-it-was. His force punched through the sphere without affecting its trajectory and, before he had a second chance, it struck him.

His shield prevented him from being seriously injured. But then he realized what it was: it was a huge ball of manure. He was now coated with and half buried in manure. His outrage went incandescent.

"You sneaky, tricky ... DEMON," he subvocalized at her. He sensed her amusement, but then another one appeared and he tried again to deflect it but, once again, his effort just punched through it and he got smashed again with a giant ball of manure. He dragged himself out of a huge pile of manure, spitting it out of his mouth and wiping it off his head.

"This is just cow manure," she subvocalized to him cheerfully. "But if I start to run out, I could switch to using pig manure." And then she lobbed another one.

Rather than punching with force, he tried to use less force, to spread the force out, and to sweep it to one side. This was more successful but still resulted in a broad swath of manure splattering all over him, even as the bulk of it was pushed to the side.

"Well done!" Tseluna said, encouragingly. "That's the first step. But, now let me push you a little: try to move the whole ball over so it stays together."

Rory tried again and again over the afternoon to spread the force out and make fine-grained adjustments to gently shift the trajectory of the whole ball rather than just smashing it.

Finally, Tseluna declared his performance adequate and with a sudden twist in his gut, they were standing by a pool of water at the base of an immense waterfall.

"Go ahead and wash up," she said.

He gratefully stripped off his filthy clothes and stepped into the pool. It was cold, but felt wonderful on a hot summer day. He waded out under the waterfall, which was frigid, but refreshing. He rinsed his hair and the rest of himself, scrubbing to try to get all the manure off.

Finally, when he started to shiver, he emerged from the waterfall and shook the water out of his hair as he waded back to the shore where Tseluna waited in the sunlight and handed him a towel.

"Where did this come from?" he asked.

"Your house," she said. "I got you some fresh clothes too."

"Thank you," he said, still shivering.

He dried off and pulled on his clean clothes.

"You did well," Tseluna said. "I think you deserve a reward."

She went to give him a kiss then recoiled.

"What?"

"You still smell like manure," she said, wrinkling up her nose. "I'll … I'll give you your reward later."

•　　　•　　　•

That night, and several showers later, Rory and Tseluna were lying together in bed.

"I still don't understand," Rory said.

"Hmm?"

"If you're a super-powerful demon, why do you hang out with people anyway?"

She sighed and looked at him. Rory stared with fascination into her unsettling, bright yellow eyes.

"I don't know exactly," she said. "After I quit the D-Force, I spent a long time just exploring low-magic dimensions. And I started encountering dimension after dimension with people. That led me to Japan and I spent a lot of time there. And … I don't know. People are interesting."

"Are we like insects to you?"

"Maybe a little," she admitted. "But to say that you're just pets isn't right either."

"I was going to ask," he said. "I mean, you don't usually have sex with pets."

"But you know what the difference is, don't you?"

Rory shook his head.

"Consent," she said. "Pets can't give consent."

"But how can I consent with this collar on?" he asked, gesturing at his neck.

"Oh, that's totally different because I can read your mind."

"And that makes it okay? That you can imagine you know that I would give consent even without the collar?"

"Would you like me to make a few copies of you to test my hypothesis?"

"No, no, no," he said hastily, but then reconsidered. "Although ... Would that mean I could have multiple simultaneous experiences of ..."

"No," she said.

"Okay, okay," Rory said, looking down. "But if demons don't even have sex, then what does it mean when you kiss me? Isn't this all just a game to you?"

Tseluna reached over and took Rory's chin and lifted it up until he was meeting her gaze again.

"This is not just a game to me," she said. "You are not just a toy or a pet. You are important to me. You are not just a means to an end."

"But ..." he started to object but then she kissed him and wouldn't let him speak. Afterward, he pressed himself up against her in the dark and contentedly drifted off to sleep.

19

AN UNFAMILIAR PROCESS
(7 TRALONGS)

"T HE TOURNAMENT STARTS in about a week," Tseluna said. "And there are two tasks we need to accomplish."

Rory, in *seiza* position, looked up from his meditation.

"First, I need to register you for the tournament before the deadline. And second, you need to qualify."

"Register? Is that like filling out some paperwork?"

"Nothing so simple," she said. "The judges will inspect you to ensure you are a natural familiar and not something constructed. They will also mind probe you to ensure that your memories have not been tampered with and that your training has only lasted for the permitted period of time."

"Inspect? Mind probe?" Rory said with a grimace. "Is this going to be like getting a physical? This isn't going to be like the demon dimension again, is it?"

"No. Nothing like that. Since we are being entirely aboveboard, it should be nothing more than a formality. And you're used to me prowling around inside your memories, so this won't be much different."

Tseluna opened a portal, took Rory's hand, and led him through. They arrived in front of a gigantic coliseum. It was situated in an enormous city that put even Japan to shame. Rory would have liked to look longer, but Tseluna was brisk for business. She led him in through the main entrance, but then down a vast side gallery thirty or forty feet wide and sixty or seventy feet high. Eventually, they reached a line that Rory perceived was composed of pairs of trainers and familiars. The line stretched on around the curve of the coliseum, so it was impossible to tell how far back they were from the head.

"Now, we wait," Tseluna said.

The familiars were extremely diverse and, well, unfamiliar. He could see a familiar—he assumed it was the familiar—that looked like what he might call a giant snake or legless-lizard. It was a large serpentine creature, anyway. There were others that looked vaguely ape-ish. Some looked like very large insects. One was a giant humanoid creature that didn't quite reach the ceiling, but couldn't have laid down crosswise in the gallery. The trainers ... Rory put on his sunglasses that let him visualize magic.

"Are the trainers *all* demons?" Rory asked.

"Pretty much," Tseluna admitted. "I've seen others compete before, but it's rare. I don't see any trainers here that aren't demons."

They waited while the line moved slowly forward. Over time, more trainers and familiars arrived behind them. Eventually, they reached a door. Tseluna made his collar visible, spoke to an attendant in her horrifying demon language of clicks and trills, then handed his leash to the attendant. Rory felt his connection to Tseluna vanish.

"Wait! What? What's happening?" Rory asked in genuine panic.

"I'm not allowed to go in while they examine you to ensure I don't influence the observations."

He dug in his feet for a moment and then heard a loud strange voice in his head.

"RESISTANCE WILL BE PUNISHED."

He quit resisting and followed docilely. He was taken into a large room where he looked around at dozens of monstrous creatures being inspected.

"DO NOT INSPECT OTHER ENTRANTS."

He quit looking around and instead focused on the demon leading him to a spot near the wall. There were two other demons there.

"Do I need to ..." Rory started to ask.

"DO NOT MAKE UNNECESSARY SOUNDS."

Rory was conducted over to the wall, where the other two demons waited. They turned their attention to him and suddenly he felt like he was very small and they were towering over him. He realized they were starting to mind-probe him. Without really meaning to, he tried to wall them off from himself, to protect his most private thoughts and feelings.

Overwhelming agony broke out over his whole body and he screamed.

"RESISTANCE WILL BE PUNISHED."

After an eternity, the agony stopped and he curled into himself internally and let the demons pore over his memories. He could hear them discussing various things, but couldn't understand them. Some of their comments sounded like laughter to him, but he was too terrified to even consider taking umbrage. Any time not spent in agonizing pain was enough for the moment.

"REMOVE YOUR CLOTHING."

Rory promptly stripped off his shirt, pants, shoes, and socks.

"REMOVE YOUR CLOTHING," the demon repeated.

Beet red, Rory removed his underwear and stood entirely naked in the giant room filled with demons and monsters. The demons minutely inspected his entire body. Once again, he detected what sounded like laughter and stood miserably while the demons made sport of his appearance.

"RETURN TO YOUR OWNER."

Rory gathered up his clothing and was walked back out the door to Tseluna. The other demon handed his leash back to Tseluna. When his bond with Tseluna was restored, he nearly fainted with relief. He felt her briefly inspect his memories and then she pulled him into a hug.

"Good boy," she said. "You did very well." He broke down into tears as she hugged him and patted his back.

"I'm sorry you had to go through that," she said. "That was probably my fault for teaching you to resist mind probes."

"No," Rory said, wiping his eyes. "It's these horrible demons who treat people like animals. How can they even talk to me? They don't speak my language, do they?"

"Mind-to-mind communication usually occurs at a level below language, so language is less important."

She waited patiently while he dressed. Then she led him farther along the gallery. After a bit, they found themselves waiting in another line.

"One thing might help you understand the circumstances a bit better," Tseluna said. "Though it does not excuse their behavior. You should know that most of the familiars really cannot be reasoned with. Most of the demons plan to use their familiar as a puppet. Their 'training' of a familiar is really about training themselves to control the familiar and has nothing to do with teaching the familiar anything."

"You mean ..."

"That's right. For most demons, this tournament is like playing a video game."

"What is a video game?" Rory asked.

"Oh, right. I'll ... I'll show you sometime—after your training is complete."

They waited in line until it was their turn to enter the arena for the qualifying examination. They entered the empty coliseum. Other than a small panel of observers, the seats were empty. Standing in the middle was a demon with a small, green monster wearing a familiar collar.

"What's that?" he subvocalized to Tseluna.

"You can call it a goblin," she said. "It's a very weak monster. It will present no real challenge to you."

"What am I supposed to do here?" Rory asked.

"The referees will make a distinctive trill and then you need to defeat the opponent."

"Do I need to kill it?"

"You can. But you don't have to."

Rory thought about it. He prepared a small amount of magical power and held himself in readiness.

He heard the trill and Tseluna said, "Go!" Rory silently reached out and tried to stroke its hypothalamus, but discovered the goblin didn't have one.

"It doesn't have a hypothalamus!" he subvocalized to Tseluna as the goblin charged him.

"No, the anatomy is different," she replied. "Here!" And she put an image in his mind's eye that showed where to stroke.

In a panic, with the goblin nearly upon him, he grabbed some magical power, reached out, and spoke the word of power. The goblin's head exploded, spraying him with blood and bits of tissue.

The panel of observers conferred and a demon made a different trill.

"Unanimous Decision: Rory," Tseluna translated and he felt a little bump of pleasure.

"You're not going to punish me for speaking the word of power?"

"We're not training anymore," she said. "You won and that's the important thing in a battle. Here's your ... reward ..."

She pulled him into an embrace, then began to lick his face clean with her rough tongue. He struggled for a moment, blushing, until he finally gave up, relaxed, and let her have her way with him.

"Good boy," she said, patting his head. "As soon as you're ready you start the next qualifying bout."

"I'm ready," he said.

She spoke to the referee with a series of clicks and trills. The referee gestured and another trainer with a hulking gray familiar took the field.

"Let me guess," Rory said. "This is a troll."

"Sure," she said. "That's as good a name as any. They're very tough and have high resistance to magical attacks."

"How are they at flying?" Rory asked, already beginning to collect magical energy.

"Huh?" Tseluna started to say when the trill announcing the beginning of the match began and Rory released the magical energy to throw the troll hundreds of feet up in the air. After some seconds it came down sideways with a loud crunch. It twitched feebly a few times and Rory heard the trill announcing the end of the match.

"The first two opponents are to check that you're minimally able to defend yourself. But the next is supposed to help assess your actual abilities," Tseluna advised. "So this is not going to be a walk-over like the other two."

Rory watched as a demon came out leading a dragon on familiar leash.

"A dragon?" he said. "Really?"

"Yes," Tseluna said. "They are extremely intelligent, long-lived, and powerful. They're headstrong as familiars, but popular with certain kinds of trainers."

"Hmm. Can you tell if they're being ... What was the word you used? Puppeted?"

"Good question," Tseluna said, looking more carefully. "I can't be certain, but I think they are not being ... puppeted. I like that word."

"Interesting," Rory said. "Are dragons as curious as they are in our myths?"

"Oh, my! Yes. If anything, even more so."

"Okay. I'm ready."

Tseluna signaled the observers and they made the trill that started the match. Rory and the dragon stepped forward.

Rory looked at the dragon and suddenly broke into hysterical laughter. The dragon paused, looked around, and Rory heard in his head a booming voice.

"What's so funny?"

"Oh, that thing on your head!" he said. "I've never seen something so funny."

"There is nothing on my head," the dragon said. "You're making it up."

"What *is* that?" Rory asked, roaring with laughter, and holding his belly. "Is that a flower? It's so cute! Look in a mirror. I can't fight you like this!"

The dragon swiped at its head ineffectually.

"Here. Can I help?" Rory said. The dragon reached its head down toward Rory.

Rory, who had been building up as much magical energy as he dared, pressed his hand against the dragon's head, raised his shield, and emitted the most powerful lightning bolt known to man. The dragon jerked violently and then started thrashing wildly, sending Rory and Tseluna—and the other trainer—backpedaling to avoid being crushed. The dragon smashed against the wall below the observers and knocked them all out of their seats. After a few moments, the dragon settled down to just some periodic twitches, but seemed to be otherwise unconscious.

The observers trilled, marking the end of the bout.

Tseluna picked Rory up and spun him around in her arms.

"Good boy! Very well done indeed!"

"I think that guy's going to have a headache in the morning," Rory said.

After Rory was certified as a qualified familiar for the tournament, Tseluna opened a portal and took his hand to bring him home.

20

AN UNFAMILIAR HEAT

(5 TRALONGS)

ON A BRUTALLY HOT SUMMER DAY, after Rory got back from his run, he found Tseluna lying naked on the floor. She was usually naked, so that wasn't so much of a surprise. But it was weird to see her on the floor (when she wasn't being a kitten).

Rory, being the master of subtlety, asked, "Why are you lying on the floor?"

"It's soooooo hot," she said.

"Oh!" Rory groused. "Sure. You're just lying around here. How do you think I feel after you sent me out into the heat to run!"

"You're young," she said. "You can take it. When you get old, like me, it's a lot harder to deal with the heat."

"I'm getting into the shower," he said, rolling his eyes.

Fifteen minutes later, he was much refreshed after a cool shower. He pulled on fresh clothes and regarded his erstwhile "owner"—as the demons had put it—still lying on the floor.

"Maybe you should take a cool shower," he suggested.

"I don't wanna," she said.

"I'm not sure how to help you," he said. "If walking two steps into the bathroom is too much work."

Just then, Rory heard the bells of an ice-cream cart going by outside.

"Hey! That's an idea. Do you want to get some ice cream?"

"What?" she said, perking up. "That sounds wonderful. Let's go!"

By the time they hit the door, Tseluna had transformed into "Sunny," her younger human persona.

"You're not going to be a kitten?" Rory asked.

"If I was a kitten, you'd probably only give me a tiny lick!"

"Whatever," Rory said, rolling his eyes.

By the time they were outside, the cart had moved out of sight, but they could still hear the music, so they ran in that direction.

Around the corner, Rory caught a glimpse of the cart as it turned at the next corner, but then he saw a little girl standing by a tree crying.

"Wait! Wait!" he said to Tseluna.

He walked over to the little girl.

"What's wrong?" Rory asked.

"My kitty climbed up the tree and can't get down," she sobbed. "And she's so hot she's panting!"

"What's your kitty's name?" Rory asked.

"Nyancy," the girl said.

"I'll get Nyancy down," Rory said.

"I can just cut the tree down," Tseluna subvocalized, angrily, watching the ice cream cart vanish around the corner.

"We can catch up," Rory replied, as he began to shinny up the tree.

Rory shinnied until he reached the lowest branch, then got a knee over the branch and began to climb in earnest. He reached the upper branches and was able to get ahold of the cat and pull it to his chest. Then he climbed down to the lower branches then jumped to the ground.

"Here you go!" he said, handing Nyancy to the little girl. She beamed with pleasure.

"Thank you, mister!" she said, running back toward her house.

"I think that's the first time someone's called me mister," Rory said, puffing himself up.

"C'mon, c'mon!" Tseluna said. "Let's go!"

They started trotting again, turned the corner and could see the cart at some distance now turning into the park.

"There it is!" she said. She and Rory ran under the blazing sun and turned into the park. Rory could see the cart down by the pavilion. But as they went down the hill, Rory heard another child crying. He turned off and went down the slope next to the sidewalk to where a boy was standing in tears.

"What's wrong?" he asked.

"I can't find my mommy!" the boy wailed.

"He lives on Chestnut street," Tseluna said. "Let's just send him back there."

"No!" Rory said, scowling at her. "He probably came here with his mom. She's probably here someplace looking for him."

"What's your name?" Rory asked the boy.

"Walter."

"Were you playing on the playground with your mom, Walter?" he asked.

"Yeah?"

"Let's go see if your mom is still by the playground."

Rory took his hand and they trooped over to the other side of the pavilion and Rory perceived a woman who was wringing her hands and looking all around. Rory waved and pointed down at Walter. The woman shrieked and came running. When Walter spotted her, he started running too. When they met, she picked him up and hugged him. Rory and Tseluna ambled over.

"Oh, you found my Walter!" she said. "Thank you so much! I was so worried."

"You're very welcome," Rory said, then turned and led Tseluna back to the pavilion.

"In the meantime," Tseluna groused. "The cart is gone again, already."

"We'll find it," Rory said. They spent a minute cooling off in the shade and drinking cool water from the drinking fountain.

They climbed the steep hill out of the park, listening for the tinkling music of the cart. Rory thought he heard it to the right, so they headed in that direction. After a few minutes, however, they discovered that he was hearing someone's wind chimes, so they turned away and headed back toward the center of town. Tseluna was bitter and unforgiving about him losing the cart and pouted angrily.

"I'm sorry," Rory said, carefully. "I'm sure we'll find it soon."

"But will they even have any left?" Tseluna grumped.

"There they are!"

Near the town green, Rory heard the jingly music again and they ran across the green toward where they could see the cart heading into a neighborhood on the other side.

As they followed it into the neighborhood, Rory heard yet another child crying and turned up a sidewalk to where a girl was crying outside a door.

"No!" Tseluna said, exasperated. But Rory ignored her and walked up the sidewalk to talk to the girl.

"What's wrong?" he asked.

"I locked myself out," she said. "I need to use the bathroom, but I can't get in."

"Oh. That's a problem," Rory said. "Do your parents leave a key outside?"

"I don't know," she said, tearing up again.

"Don't worry," Rory said. "We'll think of something. Maybe there's a window open that I could ..."

Before he could finish talking, the little girl vanished.

"C'mon!" Tseluna said.

"What did you do to her?" Rory asked, shocked. "Did you really just te..."

Then the door opened and the little girl peeked out.

"Thank you!" she said.

"Come! On!" Tseluna said, pulling Rory's shirt. They sprinted down the street and finally caught up with the ice-cream cart.

"What would you like?" the man said, finally stopping.

"I'll have a scoop of sweet cream," Rory said, then turned to Tseluna. "What would you like?"

"I'll have four," she said.

"Four what?" he asked.

"Iced spleens," she said. "Four iced spleens, please."

"They don't have iced spleens," Rory said, after he got over his momentary shock. "They just have ice cream."

"What?"

"They have ice cream. Not iced spleens. Those sound extremely nasty."

"Have you ever had any?"

"Well, no," Rory said. "But neither has anyone else. I refuse to believe that iced spleens are a thing."

"Ah. Well," she said. "If you're ignorant of the pleasures of iced spleens then there's just nothing to be done for you."

"You're crazy," Rory said in disbelief. "You've never had any 'iced spleens' either."

"Ah!" she said. "Do you want to wager?"

"What?" Rory said.

"Do you want to bet?" Tseluna said. "What are you willing to wager that I've never had iced spleens?"

"Oh, no," Rory said. "No, no, no. I'm not willing to bet on something like that. Who knows what nasty, crazy things you've done in the past?"

"Well, okay," she said. "Be that way. But you don't get to say I've never had them before."

"Okay," he said. "I won't say that you've never had them before. But you can't have them here either. So what do you want?"

"Oh, I guess I'll have some ice cream then. You're getting sweet cream? Why don't I get the same thing."

"One scoop?"

"Okay."

Rory accepted his scoop of ice cream from the man, passed it to Tseluna and requested another for himself. Then he paid the man and they took their ice cream over to a nearby bench and sat in the shade. Tseluna took a lick of her ice cream and pronounced it good—though still not, she claimed, as good as iced spleens.

"It must be fun to sell ice cream in the summer," Rory said. "Maybe I should get an ice-cream cart and do that."

"There's already an ice cream cart," Tseluna pointed out. "Maybe you should get an iced spleen cart so you wouldn't have any competition."

"How about this," Rory said. "Why don't I get an ice cream cart and you can sell iced spleens—if anyone wants to buy them."

"Nah. I'd probably just eat them all myself," she said.

•   •   •

In the afternoon, Tseluna teleported them to a remote alpine meadow—where it was cool—and helped Rory, yet again, practice how to tweak his fireball and lightning bolt spells. He could now make fireballs that could explode and ball lightning that could go around corners or go around to attack an enemy from behind. While he was practicing, however, a question occurred to him.

"Why aren't you teaching me more spells?" he asked.

"Like what?"

"I don't know. I just thought you were going to teach me more spells and not just have me keep practicing the ones I know."

"Well, here's the thing. I know vast numbers of spells, but most of them are not suitable for the tournament. Do you really want to 'talk to plants' or 'purify water'?"

"I guess those wouldn't help much in the tournament. But aren't there spells that would let me conjure an ally to fight with me?"

"There are, but those spells are also forbidden in the tournament. There are a bunch of things that are forbidden in the tournament. Weapons for example. So spells that enhance weapons are pointless."

"I can see that."

"Then there are a bunch of spells that relate to your opponent's mind. Mind probe. And confusion—stuff like that, right?"

"Right! Why are you not teaching me those?"

"If a familiar is being puppeted—your word—it doesn't help to confuse it. Because the demon who's controlling it isn't confused."

"Oh. I guess I can see that."

"The same with 'fear' and 'geas' and all those other spells. They won't have any effect."

"Oh."

"Similarly, there are a bunch of spells like 'illusion' and 'fog' that might work on the familiar's senses, but probably would have no effect on the demon. And there are whole reams of spells that just aren't relevant. Like healing. Or repair. Or necromancy. None of that would help you win."

"I guess not."

"Finally," Tseluna said. "As a novice, you're better off not having too many choices. It's easy to get paralyzed trying to decide what to do. If you only have a few choices, there's less risk of that."

"I guess you've thought about this some," Rory admitted.

"Oh! Hey! There's also familiar magic!" Tseluna said. "I don't think it would help you, but it might just help me win!"

"Ha, ha," Rory said with disgust.

She laughed and slapped his back.

21

UNFAMILIAR PERILS
(2 TRALONGS)

RORY WAS HEADED TO THE STORE to buy groceries for dinner when felt a sudden unfamiliar shift in his equilibrium and found himself teleported. He was in absolute darkness. One of the first spells every student learned was to make light. He silently called up a tiny light and looked around.

"It's that pesky demon," Tseluna subvocalized to him.

"I seem to be inside some kind of glass sphere or bubble," Rory said. "Underground, maybe?"

"Yes, I can see where you are. Be very cautious," Tseluna said. "Don't take any rash actions. Don't try to force your way out—it might backfire on you. Just sit very still and try to stay calm. Conserve your oxygen."

"Maybe you should take them more seriously this time."

"I will take it under advisement."

"Still, this has to be some kind of trap," Rory told her. "And I'm the bait. So please be careful."

"You worry too much," she said. "This demon can't store magic. They're using a device—kind of like SCUBA gear—to provide magic while they're here. But it's not enough to be a serious worry."

"What is 'SCUBA gear'?" Rory asked, puzzled.

"It's ... Never mind. I'll tell you another time."

Rory sat down and tried to stay calm, but his heart kept pounding. Eventually he realized he could do meditation practice and he got into *seiza* position and began to meditate. He focused and calmed himself down. He brought his breathing under control and his heart rate dropped.

A shock hit the glass bubble and knocked him over. Then a series of repeated shocks bounced him around inside. The glass began to fragment and little slivers of glass began to fall on him.

"What's happening?" he subvocalized to Tseluna.

When there was no immediate answer, he began to worry.

"Are you okay?" he said, panic setting in.

"Hang on," she said.

There was another shock. Then another. And then a really big shock that literally bounced him off the ceiling. His hands and knees were getting cut up and picking up glass splinters. He was now in full panic mode, hyperventilating and trying to cover his head. But, trapped in the bubble, all he could do was whimper.

Light appeared at the top of the bubble and then Tseluna broke open the top of the bubble and teleported him out.

The heat hit him first. He found himself standing on a sweltering, desolate plane of fused glass. It appeared she had teleported him while leaving all the glass fragments behind. Myriad tiny cuts on his hands and knees began to bleed freely. Far off in the distance, in every direction, he could see smoke and flames and, above him, there was a huge plume of smoke that rose to a gigantic cloud far, far overhead.

Rory looked at Tseluna with shock.

"Well, you said to go all out," she said, shrugging.

Rory began hopping as the heat from the ground started making his shoes smolder.

"Ouch, ouch, ouch!" he said, beginning a little dance hopping from foot to foot.

"Let's go home," Tseluna said and teleported them back.

After Tseluna helped patch him up, he went a second time to the store and finally bought some groceries for dinner. Rory hurriedly prepared dinner anticipating the arrival of his father. He had prepared a light meal of fresh salad and sliced chicken breast. Once he had set the table, however, he was puzzled at how late his father was getting home.

He was looking at the clock when he heard a THUD against the door. When he opened the front door, no-one was there, but there was a rock on the stoop with a paper wrapped around it, tied up with string. He untied the string and read the paper.

"We have your father. Come alone if you ever want to see him again."

There was an address provided.

"I'm getting tired of this shit," Rory said, throwing the rock angrily down by the door. "Can I just give them what they're asking for?"

"Yes," Tseluna said. "Yes, I think you should. I think you can deal with them as you see fit."

They walked across town to the address with Tseluna in kitten form. He walked up to the door with Tseluna perched on his shoulder. It was a large house, well cared for, with a wide lawn. He walked up to the front and knocked on the door. The door opened and a large man with an ill-favored expression looked at him, then turned and called back.

"It's the kid!"

Rory couldn't hear the response from indoors, but the goon directed him to come in and led him into a sitting room. There were four or five men surrounding his father who was blindfolded and tied to a chair in the middle of the room. In the back of the room, sitting in an easy chair, was a heavyset man with a large gold chain around his neck.

"So good of you to join us," he said. "I've been wanting to speak with you. You've been getting in our way and … interfering. Yeah. Interfering. Before, I was just going to give you a little warning and tell you to back off. But now you've been so much trouble that I think you owe us more. You work for me now."

"I think the time for conversation is over," Rory said.

"You can say goodbye to your father then," the man said gesturing at one of his henchman who drew a knife and went to put it to his father's throat. Rory lit up shields both around himself and around his father. The goon stepped forward and bounced off Rory's shield. He couldn't approach closer than two or three feet. They looked among themselves unsure how to proceed.

Rory gathered magic energy and silently released a gigantic fireball. It was not the biggest he'd ever made, but it was significantly larger than the house and it blasted the house off its foundations and tore it to flaming fragments that scattered over the whole neighborhood. Rory was left standing amid the smoking ruins with his father sitting inside a bubble on a perfect circle of undamaged carpet. Everyone else was parboiled with charred extremities. Then the bodies all vanished.

"Did you do that?" Rory subvocalized to Tseluna.

"Yes," she replied. "There's no sense in leaving behind evidence. You never asked, but I did the same with the bodies of the men who attacked you on the bridge."

"Do I want to know what you do with them?" Rory asked.

"Probably not."

Rory shrugged. Then he dropped the shields, walked over, removed his father's blindfold, and released him from the chair.

"Rory!" he said, then looked around in astonishment. "What happened? Did you do this? What did you do?"

"C'mon, Dad. Let's go home before the constables come," Rory said, pulling him to his feet.

They walked away as people were still coming out of their houses to see what had happened. The constables ran past them as they walked casually along.

"How did you do that?" Rory's dad asked.

"This is what I've been training for," Rory said, simply. "I've learned a lot with Mrs. T's coaching."

"Learned a lot ..." mused Rory's dad. "I had no idea you could do anything like this. I've never even heard of *anyone* who could do anything like that."

"Well, I leave for the tournament tomorrow," Rory said. "Hopefully I've learned enough."

"Oh, you've got this in the bag," he said, tousling Rory's hair. Rory grinned.

22

AN UNFAMILIAR NIGHT

(1 TRALONG)

R ORY AWOKE EARLY in the morning the day before the tournament. Tseluna was standing next to his bed wearing the bright, colorful robe she had worn when they met with Hideyoshi-san.

"What's up?" Rory asked.

"You have completed your training," she said. "Today, I thought I would take you someplace special where you can relax before the big day."

"I'll get ready."

"You should also say goodbye to your father," she said. "Because, afterward, we will go straight to the tournament."

"Oh, right," Rory said.

After putting his clothes on, Rory went to the dining room where his dad was drinking coffee and reading the newspaper.

"Mrs. T and I are leaving today for the tournament," Rory said.

"That's so exciting!" his dad said. "I'll be interested to hear all about it when you get home."

It wasn't until this moment that Rory realized that this might be—even probably would be—the last time he saw his father. He choked up a bit, but leaned over and gave his father a big hug.

"Yeah, Dad," Rory said, tearing up. "Yeah. I'll tell you all about it when I get home."

When he got back to his room, he looked around.

"Do I need to pack?" he asked.

"That won't be necessary," Tseluna said. Then she waved her hand and opened a portal. She reached over to him.

"Are you ready?"

Rory took one last look at his room, then at Tseluna.

"If … If the worst comes to pass, will you promise to return and explain to my father what happened?"

She looked at him and smiled gently.

"Yes," she said. "I promise. Now stop being so maudlin and let's go have fun."

Rory took her hand and stepped through the portal.

They stepped out onto a rocky shoreline. Huge waves crashed against jagged rocks and a cool breeze blew a salty mist onto their faces. Rory took a deep breath smelling the crisp, clean sea air.

"It's beautiful," Rory said, in wonder.

"Would you like to stroll along the shore?"

"Do we have time?"

"We have the whole day," Tseluna said. "You should enjoy yourself to the fullest."

Hand-in-hand, they walked along a narrow strip of black sand between the waves and the rocks. In places, the rocks came down to the water and they stopped to look into the tide pools full of fish and limpets and sea urchins.

"What's that red thing?" Rory asked.

"That's a sea star," Tseluna said. "I am given to understand that they eat clams."

Rory turned and looked out over the ocean.

"What's on the other side of the sea?"

"Eventually, there is another continent."

"Is that also Japan?"

"No," Tseluna said. "There are actually many human states on the planet. We were in a different one when we visited Death Valley."

"Oh."

"These days, I mostly stay in Japan," she said. "But about a million tralongs ago, I made the mistake of visiting other parts of the planet. I found that culturally they weren't ready for things like demons and, well, let's just say it generated some misunderstandings ..."

"Why is this world so much like my world?" Rory asked. "It can't be a coincidence that people here are so much like the people on my world."

"It cannot," Tseluna said. "I believe that someone or something seeded the living things from here across many dimensions."

"How many dimensions have you visited?"

"Thousands," Tseluna said. "Maybe tens of thousands. As I told you before, most dimensions are lifeless. But this place is special too. It's so magic poor that the people here have had to find a million different ways to do things. It's a fascinating place."

"How long have you been visiting my dimension?" Rory asked. Tseluna looked at him. "I know you must have been coming for a long time because you knew that piece of ancient literature."

"You're pretty sharp," Tseluna said. "Yes. I've visited your dimension for many thousands of tralongs. Not often and never for very long."

Rory watched the waves.

"Why did you pick me?"

"There were many reasons. You were the right age. You could already make a shield. You wanted battle magic so badly. You were hurting with the loss of your mother. But, most of all, you were kind to a kitten. And you were sad when you thought the kitten was hurt. And when you stood over me to face down a direwolf ..." Tseluna pulled him into a hug.

"Oh, Rory! You've shown me over and over again that I made the right choice," Tseluna said. "You've worked so hard and learned so much. You will make a great champion.

"Now," she said. "Let's go check in and have lunch."

"Check in?" Rory asked.

Tseluna turned him so he was looking away from the ocean and close at hand was a large, low building with a curved, tiled roof. There were huge windows and clouds of steam rising from behind.

"Come!" she said, drawing him forward.

When they reached the building, Rory nearly jumped out of his skin when the doors suddenly slid to the side automatically. There were unfamiliar lights with quiet atmospheric music playing in a broad lobby area. Rory could see through to the other side of the building where large colorful moving objects were visible through the doors.

"More of those vehicles?" he asked.

"Yes. I can show you later, if you like. For now, let's get checked in."

They walked up to the counter and Tseluna spoke a few words in Japanese. The staff immediately struck a look of solemn reverence.

"*Irasshaimase*, Tseluna-sama!" a woman said, and immediately led them down a long hallway to the very end where she opened a door and bowed deeply. Tseluna spoke again, evidently thanking her, and led Rory inside.

"They know you here?"

"I should hope so," she said. "After all, I'm the owner."

"What?"

"Well, my ownership of this *onsen* is via a legal entity that Hideyoshi-san and I created many years ago. But it amounts to the same thing."

She flipped a switch on the wall that turned the lights on like magic. Then she led Rory around the room showing him the amenities. In a closet, she pulled out two robes and gave one to Rory. "Change into this kimono—it's more comfortable."

There was a quiet tap on the door as he was tying the sash around himself. Tseluna opened the door and a waitress carried in a large platter and placed it on a low table. On the platter were small, colorful bite-sized viands.

"Come have some sushi," Tseluna said. "*Itadakimasu!*"

"*Itadakimasu!*" he repeated, as best as he could. He pointed at some green stuff. "What's this?"

"Ah. That's wasabi," she said. "It has a very strong flavor, so be cautious."

He tried a tiny taste and rejected it utterly which made Tseluna laugh. But then he tried the sushi and was amazed by the complex synthesis of tastes and textures.

"What is this?" he asked.

"Raw fish, mostly."

"Raw fish?" he said, looking slightly green.

"It's good though, isn't it?"

"It is," he admitted, trying another one.

After lunch, Tseluna invited him to step through a glass door which led outside to a small patio surrounded by a lovely garden with a large, sunken pool of hot water that had steam rising from it. Beyond, they could see the ocean. A strong cool breeze came off the sea.

"We should shower first to clean ourselves. Then we can soak in the hot spring."

She took him into the bathroom, turned on the shower, and pulled him in with her. She opened a tiny bottle and lathered him up with shampoo from head to toe.

"Whoa! It smells like oranges!" he said.

Tseluna let Rory wash her as well. He was used to seeing her naked body, but not touching her. His breathing deepened as he ran his hands over her shoulders, her belly and back, her thighs and calves. He finally found himself on his knees washing her feet and blushing because of where his face was.

After they stepped out of the shower, Rory discovered there was a door directly out from the bathroom to the patio. They walked carefully over and stepped into the hot tub. It took a few tries to get all the way down into the water because it was so hot, but then he leaned back and looked up at the sky. Being naked outside, under the sun, felt naughty, and he blushed again.

Tseluna sat next to him, then slipped her arm around his shoulders and pulled him closer to her. He leaned up against her and sighed.

"Thank you," he said. "Even if I don't survive tomorrow, I count myself lucky to have met you and to have experienced so many things that I never could have without you."

"Let me give you one more experience," she said, turning her head and pressing her mouth to his. He welcomed her rough tongue into his mouth and he put his arms around her and pulled her against him.

She stood and encouraged him to step up and then sit on the edge of the pool. His heart began to pound as he shifted. He looked up at her face as she stood over him. She offered him her breasts, while she reached down and gently squeezed and stroked his penis. He gasped when she finally lowered herself down all the way onto him and, after a few moments, began to rock back and forth. Rory moaned, overwhelmed by the physical sensations of lovemaking. He realized Tseluna had broadened the mind-to-mind connection they shared and he was feeling her pleasure directly as she shared in his. She began to move slowly at first, speeding up until he was close, and then backing off. She built his stimulation higher and higher until, bucking and shuddering, she brought him to a mindblowing peak and ultimately offered him release in a crescendo.

They stayed wrapped together for several long moments, then she pulled him back down into the water and cuddled up against him. He relaxed in her embrace, wrung out and sated.

They made love twice more that afternoon on their futon. The first time, Tseluna let Rory be on top and it was over in mere moments. The second time, she pushed him onto his back, mounted him, brought him to the brink, and held him there, quivering, until he was nearly mad with desire—and only then finally let him climax. Afterward, exhausted, they laid tangled together and napped until dinner time.

"Would you like to eat in again? Or should we go to the dining room?"

"I'm easy," he said. "What would you like to do?"

She tousled his hair.

"I want to show you off."

They showered again, put their kimonos on, and walked—arm-in-arm—to the dining room where they were conducted to a special dais in the middle of the room that was reserved for Tseluna (and guests) alone. They reclined next to the low table, flirting, while the wait staff brought small plates of delicacies to sample. Rory could feel the eyes of the other diners on him but was so consumed with his desire for Tseluna that he didn't care. She fed him morsels and stroked his hair, twirling it around her fingers. He had never felt more alive or complete. Bathed in the afterglow of his first sexual experience, it was unquestionably the peak experience of his entire life. But finally, after dinner came to an end, they headed back to their room for the night.

Walking back, hand-in-hand, Tseluna paused for a moment, then took Rory into a little side room that was full of glass-fronted cases, some containing brightly colored packaging and others with variously colored bottles.

"Remember our trip to Death Valley?" she asked.

"Sure?"

She pointed at a machine with bottles.

"Is that where you got the water bottles from?"

"Yep."

"Can I have one now?"

She pulled one out of thin air and handed it to him. He heard a *ker-chunk* sound in the machine as the bottles shifted positions.

"You never cease to amaze me, my goddess."

"*Baka.*"

After they returned to their room, Rory lay in his futon for a long time, twisting and turning.

"Tseluna?" he whispered, finally.

"Hmm?"

"I'm scared," he admitted.

"It would be foolish not to be," she said. "But you've trained hard and are as well prepared as anyone could be."

"It's this ... waiting," he said, shivering. "I'm not sure I can sleep. Will you hold me?"

She rolled over and he turned and buried his head in her chest, sobbing.

"I'm sorry. I'm sorry," he kept saying.

"Ssh. It's alright. It's okay," she said, holding and patting him, gently. In the end, she let him nurse until he finally fell into a fitful sleep.

23

A FAMILIAR BATTLE

(0 TRALONGS)

T SELUNA AND RORY WALKED OUT from the underground gallery where they'd been waiting with the other contestants into the huge coliseum. The stands were filled with tens of thousands of demons with a sprinkling of other creatures of all descriptions. An announcer identified each pair of contestants as they emerged in the order according to their ranking.

Rory was ranked near the middle. He couldn't understand the announcements, but he did recognize his name and raised his hands over his head. This produced some small number of cheers, but they were soon lost in the noise raised for subsequent contestants. They took their place in the middle of the field. Once all of the contestants—a couple of hundred—were arrayed on the field, there was a series of incomprehensible announcements.

"They're welcoming the spectators," Tseluna said, summarizing the announcements. "Now they're welcoming the contestants. They're explaining the ladder of matches. Now they're directing everyone but the first two contestants and their familiars to leave the field." Rory and Tseluna returned to a long gallery inside the coliseum and began the wait for Rory's first bout.

Where they were waiting, they couldn't see the matches, but they could hear the roar of the crowd. The matches seemed to go very fast. After no more than a half hour, Tseluna alerted him that they were up. He headed for the entrance and preceded her into the arena.

Bright lights hurt his eyes as he stepped out into the open. The crowd set up a deafening roar. Rory looked across the field and saw his opponent. It was an odd looking creature, green, with a kind of shell, sort of like a turtle, but more humanoid.

"Ah," Tseluna subvocalized. "This is a 'nintu'. They're tough, with a high defense. But they're not particularly fast."

"How are they at flying?"

Rory summoned as much magical energy as he dared and prepared to trigger it. When he heard the trill beginning the match, he was stunned when the nintu vanished and suddenly reappeared only inches away, with an arm drawn back to strike. Rory released his magical stored energy at the feet of the nintu and, before it could strike, he sent it hundreds or thousands of feet into the air.

"Be cautious," Tseluna said. "If it can teleport, it can teleport itself back down. And it may try to teleport you."

"What can I do to avoid being teleported?"

"Don't let it approach. Make yourself bigger. Expand your shield."

Rory raised his shield at the same moment the nintu appeared right behind him with its arm still raised to strike. Rory was still in the process of pushing his shield out when the nintu struck, but it was met by the shield unexpectedly moving out. The resistance, coming at an unfamiliar point in the strike, threw off the nintu's blow and there was a crack as one of the bones of its forelimb fractured. It lost its balance and started to fall. Rory spun and tried to follow up with a windblade, but it vanished again.

Rory looked all over, but he couldn't see it anywhere.

"It can't just run away can it?"

"The demon is still there."

"Can I attack the demon?"

"Don't. If you do, the demon can fight back directly. You really don't want to fight the demon."

While he waited for the nintu to reappear, he began gathering magical energy.

Suddenly the nintu reappeared inside his shield bubble. Surprised, he spoke a word of power without thinking and released an enormous fireball inside the bubble as the shield dropped.

Rory felt Tseluna panic via the familiar bond when she saw the bubble fill up with fire and then vent. At the same moment his shield had dropped, he had silently brought up a new shield just around himself.

He reassured her via the familiar bond and, once the smoke cleared, he was left standing over the nintu that was now a blackened smoking corpse at his feet.

There was a huge roar of approval from the crowd. When Rory heard his name announced as the winner, he raised his arms and the crowd went wild again.

Tseluna met him as he walked off the field. She embraced him, perhaps a little longer than usual, and Rory hugged her a little tighter than normal. Then they walked back into the gallery to wait for his next bout.

"Why didn't you have me learn about the different kinds of opponents I was likely to face?" Rory asked.

"I considered it," Tseluna said. "But there are so many that it didn't seem worthwhile. There are way too many possibilities and you'd never be able to remember all of the salient details about them. I figured your time was better spent on improving your abilities and that I could simply tell you what you needed to know."

"Thank you," Rory said. "Now I'm imagining you standing over me making me memorize details about all these weird monsters and zapping me when I get them wrong."

"Would I ever do something like that though?" Tseluna said, holding a finger up.

"No! Never!" Rory said, laughing. "You would never do something like that."

"Whoops! We're back up already," Tseluna said.

Rory and Tseluna walked back onto the field to the roar of the crowd. His opponent this time was a kind of long, tan lizard. It was 10 or 15 feet long with large, unblinking eyes, a wide mouth, and bumpy skin.

"It's a 'rall'," Tseluna said. "I haven't seen one of those in a long while."

"What do they do?"

"They sometimes call them 'blink lizards' because they move so fast."

Rory listened to announcements until he heard the trill beginning the match, but before he could react, he was knocked down with the rall standing over him with a mouthful of dagger-like teeth in his face. He tried to shock it with electricity, but it had already pulled back. He started to get to his feet, when the rall knocked him over again. He tried to shoulder roll back to his feet but got knocked over yet again.

"The demon is toying with you," Tseluna said. "They are probably watching the odds change and waiting for the best moment to take you down."

Rory managed to get his feet under him, but couldn't even follow the rall with his eye. It circled around him in quick spurts of movement that he was unable to track.

"Tseluna?" he said, beginning to panic. "I'm not sure I can do this."

"Do you want me to help? To puppet you?"

"Please?"

"Let me see if I remember how to do this ..."

"Aaaah!" Rory would have said if he could have reacted fast enough when the rall suddenly charged him, but well before he could have reacted, his body pivoted and stepped sideways, toward the rall, and drove his hand solidly down onto the rall's head emitting a lightning bolt that sent its body into momentary tetanus and then a long series of jerks and twitches. A thin cloud of steam emerged from its mouth as it exhaled for the last time.

He heard the trill announcing the end of the bout and, by the time they announced his name he could raise his arms to the deafening roar of the crowd.

"I thought I was a goner," Rory said, as they walked off the field.

"Your reaction time is a physiological limitation. I can make your body react marginally faster than you can because demons are not limited by physiology."

"So, you're saying ..."

"Yes! It's magic!"

Rory cracked up laughing.

They had a longer wait this time. There were several dozen bouts and one in particular seemed to take a really long time. Rory could hear the crowd roaring with excitement and wished he could see what was happening on the field.

"Can you hear anything that's happening?" he asked.

"Oh. It's a match between two 'dynoslugs,'" Tseluna said. "They're powerful, but slow."

"Both trainers have the same kind of familiar?" Rory asked. "Is a dynoslug a typical familiar?"

"No," Tseluna said. "Really weird. I've never seen one used as a familiar. Ever. And for them to get matched up against each other? I wonder if this was some kind of gimmick or sideshow. Oh, well. It gives us a break."

Eventually, the match came to an end and the rapid pace of matches resumed until they were called again.

Rory and Tseluna walked back onto the field.

"Ew! What is that thing?" Rory said, wrinkling up his nose in disgust. His opponent was some kind of long segmented worm or centipede. Its head was undistinguished, but with a fringe of cilia or feelers.

"That is a 'magipou'," Tseluna said. "They're a magic parasite.

If they touch you, they can bleed off your magic and throw off your casting."

Rory heard the trill and promptly raised his shield. The magipou flowed toward him. Rory began to accumulate some magic to cast something—he was thinking a windblade seemed like a good first choice, when the magipou swung the back half of its body around like a whip and, although it had seemed far off, it touched him with a long filament that extended way out from its tail.

Rory nearly passed out from the shock when it drained his magic. It was like a short circuit that took down his shield and left him shaky with a kind of brainfog. Then it whipped its head forward and clamped onto his chest and it happened again—but didn't stop. He could feel the firehose of magic from Tseluna passing through him. He realized he was going to die. But for some reason, he remembered a story he'd heard once about mosquitos and he wrapped his arms and legs around the head of the magipou, opened himself wide, and poured as much magic as he could through the connection.

He could hear Tseluna shouting and the crowd was going wild. The magipou began to thrash and tried to disengage, but Rory held on for all he was worth. There was a sudden explosion and Rory was left lying on his back covered with stinking gunk and bits of exoskeleton.

"Get up! Get up!" Tseluna called to him urgently. He struggled to get his feet under him and stood. The crowd roared and he heard the trill announcing his victory. He didn't wait to hear his name called to raise his arms in victory. And then he fainted.

Tseluna caught Rory before he collapsed. He teetered at the edge of consciousness. He felt a breeze stir his hair and heard the ocean. He opened his eyes blearily and realized he was in some kind of small open shelter on a tiny island with ocean as far as the eye could see all around.

"Where are we?" he asked. "What about the tournament?"

"This is my special retreat," Tseluna said. "It's in a dimension where the time-dilation effect is ... significant."

"How long do I have?"

"Hours. Go swim to clean yourself off and then you can rest. Sleep, if you can."

Rory stripped off his filthy clothes and waded out into the ocean. The water was near body temperature and very salty. He ducked under and rinsed the goo off as best he could without soap.

"That was an inspired strategy," Tseluna said, as she laid out a bedroll she'd pulled out of a storage cabinet for him. "But I need to go recharge my store of magic: you nearly drained me dry!"

"You're going to leave the dimension? Won't that break the familiar bond?"

"It will," she said. "But I'm not worried about having to track you down and recapture you here."

"You will never ever have to worry about that."

"Here," she said, handing him a bottle of water. "You need to rinse the salt off. Then I'll give you a towel. There's more water over there if you're thirsty. I'm sorry it's warm. I'll try to bring you something to eat before we go back."

After he'd rinsed and dried, he collapsed onto the bedroll.

"I will miss you," he said, "Please be careful, Mommy."

She went to tousle his damp hair, but he was already asleep.

He woke up once to relieve himself and stepped into the bushes that surrounded the shelter. He felt painfully alone in his head without Tseluna's presence. But he was still tired, so he laid down and slept more. He awoke again when Tseluna returned.

"Are you ready?" she said. "It took me longer to refill than I expected and we need to head back almost immediately. Here—I brought you a sandwich. And clean clothes."

He gratefully wolfed down the sandwich and pulled on his fresh clothes.

"Are you going to remake the familiar bond?" he said standing and lifting his chin. She gestured at him and he breathed easier to feel his connection to Tseluna restored.

She opened the portal and reached toward him. He took her hand and they stepped through together.

They appeared back in the gallery just as the finalists were being called back out to the field. They followed in line with the others. The ranks of contestants had been winnowed down to fifty finalists. Once again, Tseluna translated the announcements for Rory and, at the conclusion of the announcements, the other contestants were directed to leave the field for the first bout.

Tseluna and Rory turned to leave when a circle of demons appeared high over the coliseum. Rory realized something was terribly wrong. The stands erupted in chaos and began to empty as demons began teleporting away. Then Tseluna grabbed her head, like she was in excruciating pain, and collapsed.

Rory took stock of himself and he realized he had been cut off from Tseluna: his familiar bond was gone. He looked around and saw that all of the other familiars were discovering that they too were suddenly free and their masters were incapacitated.

"Get back! Get back!" Rory cried, pulling at Tseluna's hand, but she was unresponsive. He scooped her up and carried her away from the others toward the wall. He spoke a word of power and brought up his shield but, cut off from Tseluna's magic, it was pathetically underpowered. There was more magic here than in his home dimension, but it was not like the immense flow of power he could normally draw from Tseluna. His shield was hardly visible and he could barely extend it beyond himself.

They emerged from the others, when pandaemonium broke out on the field. One of the dragons released a huge blast of fire, which roasted a dozen contestant pairs. The others scattered, but Rory perceived that the familiars were all attacking their former masters who were incapacitated like Tseluna. One demon went down, trampled by a huge rhinoceros-like creature. Another was grabbed by a long-armed vaguely-gorilla-like creature that snatched up its owner and began smashing them onto the ground.

"Help me, Tseluna!" Rory pleaded. "I need your magic!"

"The D-Force is here and the familiar bond is broken," she moaned, holding her head in her hands. "It's over."

"No!" Rory pleaded. "Put it back! Remake it!"

"You want to be in servitude?" she said.

"Yes!" Rory said. "I love you! I'll do anything to stay with you!"

He turned to face Tseluna, grabbed her face, and kissed her.

"Please!" he begged. She gestured and his collar and cord re-materialized. Once again, overflowing with magical power, his shield blazed white with new energy. He extended the shield over both of them. A blast of dragon fire washed over them as the dragon and its former master fought. The familiars that had already defeated their former masters began looking for other targets. When they charged toward Rory, he threw fireballs and lightning bolts to keep them pushed back.

Giant crystals began growing around the participants that remained. Rory realized he too was being encased in crystal, but he was powerless to stop it. He was conscious, but frozen. In moments, everything living that remained in the arena was encased in transparent, glowing crystal.

The team of D-Force demons appeared in the arena and fanned out among the crystals. A demon would touch a crystal and, after a moment, the creature inside would vanish and the crystal would collapse into liquid that evaporated almost before hitting the ground. A demon came up to his crystal, he felt a shift in his equilibrium, and the arena vanished.

24

A FAMILIAR FACE

(+1 TRALONG)

RORY REAPPEARED INSIDE his bedroom alone, still full of adrenaline with his heart racing. He clenched and unclenched his fists, panting. The house was silent. Tseluna was no longer connected to him and he felt her absence keenly. He collapsed onto his bed, put his arms over his head, and cried for a long time.

Everything had happened so quickly he had no idea what was going on: One minute he was in the tournament and the next he was just … home. It didn't seem real. Nothing seemed real. Had all that really happened? He felt shaky and uncertain. But, he supposed, that was hardly unexpected, given what he was going through.

He wondered what side-effects there might be from having the familiar bond broken. He didn't really know very much about familiar magic, but he'd never heard of familiars becoming unbound or what happened to them.

He looked at the clock. It was 10 in the morning on Monday. He was emotionally exhausted, but he didn't think he could rest because he was still too keyed up. So, he decided to walk to the school to see if they'd let him use the library even though it was still summer.

Rory arrived at the school building and climbed the stairs to the library. As he entered, he saw Mr. Burton's owl keeping watch.

Alerted by his familiar, Mr. Burton called to Rory from back among the bookshelves when he entered. "Mr. Soletsa! How has your summer been? How did your scholarship go?"

"I learned a lot, Mr. Burton, but ..." Rory began.

"Where's your familiar?" he asked.

"It's ... That's ... " he said, choking up. "She's gone."

"Oh, no!" Mr. Burton said and his owl hooted sadly. "Oh, I'm so sorry. That's really hard."

"So, I wanted to read more about familiar bonds," Rory continued, once he could talk again. "To understand better what I'm going through and what might happen."

"Well, the definitive text is by Pasquale," he said, coming out and walking across the library. He unlocked the special restricted shelf and pulled a book out. "This is an advanced text and isn't normally made available to students, but I think it's the most likely to help you understand what you're going through. Unfortunately, I can't let you check it out. So, you'll have to read it here."

Rory thanked Mr. Burton and took the book over to a table by the window where the light was good. While Mr. Burton worked nearby, Rory spent most of the day studying the book, which described the familiar bond in exquisite detail. In places, he found it hysterically funny to read because it described everything from the other perspective: that is, it was all about having a bond with a familiar, not being bound as a familiar. But Rory was careful to control his countenance and study the book seriously. The last chapters described a bunch of theoretical extensions and similar structures that people had considered or described in various circumstances. Finally, in the late afternoon, Mr. Burton finished his own work and chased Rory out, after locking the book back on the restricted shelf.

Dejected, Rory started walking home, but then turned off into the park where he'd first encountered Tseluna. Rather than wading across the creek, he crossed one of the bridges and followed the path into the forest where they'd fought the direwolves. He reached the site of the battle and looked down the long gap where his overpowered fireball had taken down a whole row of trees. He sighed to remember that feeling of overflowing power. And not just that.

He realized he was on the verge of tears again. He was so lonely, he wanted to die. Having Tseluna always in his head had been really uncomfortable at first, but that feeling of connection had made him feel complete in a way that he didn't think he would ever be able to achieve again—or with anyone else. He sighed and forced his feelings down. He was about to walk on again when he heard a twig snap. He spun and Tseluna was standing before him.

She was not wearing clothes, as was her wont, but there was a translucent collar affixed around her throat. She glared at him with her bright yellow eyes. She extended her hand with the cord toward him.

"Take it," she said.

"What?" he asked. "Now you want to be my familiar?"

"It's my punishment," she said, sullenly. "Either I become your familiar for your lifetime or I must accept confinement and torture for the same length of time. Just accept the bond."

"But …" he said. "Can't I just free you?"

"No, you can't," she said. "If the collar is removed, they'll hunt me down. Take it! Please!"

"Ah!" he said. "Hang on …"

He remembered one of the proposed extensions Pasquale had described and thought for a moment to figure out how to prepare the complicated spell he envisioned. Then he spoke the word of power and a translucent collar appeared around his own throat and its cord was joined to hers.

"*Baka!*" she shouted. "What have you done?"

"When I was reading about familiar magic this afternoon, I realized that this seemed possible," he said. "Now you're my familiar, but I'm your familiar too."

"That's ... What? What does that even mean?"

"We're now inextricably linked," he said. "And equal. I don't think either of us can remove this directly. Well, not until one of us dies. Then I think it just goes away."

"But that means ... Oh, no!"

"Yes! I can read your mind now! Aww ... You always liked me!"

"Don't say it like that!" she said angrily. Then quieter, reading his mind in turn, she said, "*Baka.* I missed you too."

He grabbed her under her arms, picked her up, and, whirling round and round, hugged her to him. Then he kissed her and thrust his tongue into her mouth. Her rough tongue avoided but then gingerly touched his.

"Can I still have my nummies in the morning?"

"Yes," she sighed, rolling her bright, yellow eyes. "Yes, you can still have your nummies."

25

A FAMILIAR TIME

(+2 TRALONGS)

RORY AND TSELUNA WALKED HOME conferring over how to present their new, changed circumstances to Rory's dad in a way he might understand. Rory had Tseluna hang back for a minute as they arrived home, and he found his dad putting the finishing touches on dinner for himself.

"You're back already!" his dad exclaimed. "I thought you were going to be gone for longer!"

"Well, there was a slight change in plans," Rory said. "It turns out that Tseluna is actually a demon. And … Well … We're sort of married now."

"Hi," Tseluna said, coming up from behind him. Rory put his arm around her. Rory's dad stopped what he was doing and looked back and forth between the two of them: his very ordinary son and the dark-skinned demon with brilliant yellow eyes wearing a school uniform, Tseluna's one concession to propriety.

"Married?" he said, stunned and still trying to comprehend what he was hearing. "Don't you mean 'engaged'?"

Tseluna and Rory looked at each and shook their heads.

"No," Rory said. "We mean married. I mean … not like legally or anything."

"Are you telling me you eloped?" Rory's dad said.

"That's a word! Sure. Yes. We eloped!"

"And what do the young lady's parents have to say about this?"

"Oh. I'm a demon," Tseluna said. "I've never had any parents."

"What?"

"And I'm not exactly young either," she continued.

"How old are you, exactly?"

"Dad! What kind of question is that to ask a lady?"

•   •   •

After dinner, Rory and Tseluna joined Rory's dad in the living room. He sat in his easy chair and Rory and Tseluna sat together on the couch holding hands.

"I was kind of shocked to hear you'd gotten married and I'm still trying to wrap my head around it," Rory's dad said. "I guess I'm not opposed. But I would like you to finish your schooling."

Rory looked at Tseluna, who nodded.

"It's kind of silly though," Rory said. "Because I can read Tseluna's mind and she already knows everything they're going to teach us—and more!"

"You don't know that," his dad countered.

"Actually, I do because she snuck into the school and looked at all the lesson plans."

"How else could I know how to structure your training regimen?"

"I'm not saying you shouldn't have. I'm simply establishing that we know that they're not going to teach me anything I don't already know."

"You mean that *I* don't already know."

"But it's pretty much the same thing now, isn't it?"

"I'm thinking more about your emotional maturity," his dad said. "And where is she going to sleep anyway?"

"She's been sleeping in my room for months already, Dad."

"Oh. What! You mean, like that?"

"Don't worry," Tseluna said. "I'm a demon so I don't need to sleep anyway."

"And have you given any thoughts to children?" Rory's dad asked.

Rory flushed at the change in subject and was surprised to discover that he could feel mirroring embarrassment from Tseluna via the familiar bond.

"We haven't talked about it," Rory admitted.

"Well, I know that I would love for you to have a family someday. And I'm certain your mom's parents feel the same way."

"We'll probably need to practice first," she said, leaning up against Rory and making him blush even more. "We'll probably need to practice a whole lot."

•   •   •

The next day, Tseluna attracted stares when she arrived on Rory's arm and then stood behind his chair in the classroom.

"Mr. Soletsa, who is that?" Mr. Burton asked, his owl looking quizzically, turning its head first one way and then another as he tried to call the class to order.

"This is my familiar, Tseluna," Rory explained. Tseluna grinned and waved. "I'm also her familiar," he continued.

"I thought she was a cat," Mr. Burton said.

"I thought so too, at first. But she's actually a demon."

"I thought you lost her."

"She came back," Rory replied.

"And ... Did you say you're her familiar too?"

"Yup."

"What does that even mean?"

"We're co-familiars. It's sort of like being married."

"But with less privacy," Tseluna clarified.

•   •   •

Between periods, Buck came up to Rory and Tseluna.

"So, you weren't really on Team Cat after all," he said, sadly.

"No," Rory said. "I'm sorry we deceived you."

Buck brightened.

"But you did save me. And Miri," he said, cheerfully. "I will always be very grateful. And I still think you're the best, Tseluna. It's nice to have you in class."

"Aw," she said, patting his face. "You're very sweet."

•   •   •

The moment Mr. Burton dismissed the class for lunch, Tseluna teleported Rory and herself to the cafeteria, where they were first in line.

"I'll have a roast-beef sandwich," Rory said. "And whatever this young lady would like."

"I'll have the same," she said, cheerfully. "And two bottles of milk, please!"

Once they had their sandwiches, Tseluna teleported them to Rory's bench, just as the other students were arriving at the cafeteria.

Rory was half done with his sandwich when Aimee showed up.

"How did you get here so fast?" she said.

"Magic," Rory said, his mouth full of sandwich.

"Ew," Aimee said. Then she looked at Tseluna and scowled.

"I still don't trust you," she said. "I mean, demons don't really look like that, do they?"

"Like what?"

"Like with those huge boobs."

Tseluna leaned over and beckoned to Aimee. Aimee stepped a bit closer.

"Can I let you in on a little secret?" she said in a conspiratorial whisper. "Boys like boobs."

"That's disgusting," Aimee said.

"Well, how do you think demons should look? Like this?"

Tseluna transformed and became indistinguishable from Aimee. Aimee's mouth dropped open with surprise and indignation. Tseluna stuck her tongue out at Aimee. Then inspiration struck.

"Hey, hey, hey!" Tseluna said, still looking identical to Aimee and draping her arms over Rory's shoulders. "I have a great idea for our honeymoon!"

"Oh, no!" Aimee said. "Stop it. You're going too far."

Tseluna transformed back and pouted.

"You probably shouldn't tease her so much," Rory subvocalized to Tseluna.

"But do you know what she's actually thinking?"

"Are you reading her mind too?"

"Well, she's so open."

"Hey! Now, that's not polite!" Aimee said, getting angrier, if possible.

"What?"

"Secretly talking about people behind their back!"

"How could you tell?" Rory asked.

"It's obvious!" she said, rolling her eyes. "You're both so obvious! The way you flirt all the time is scandalous! Rory Soletsa, I hate you."

Aimee flounced off in a rage.

"Just think how angry she'd be if she knew you were reading her mind too," Rory said.

"She doesn't really hate you, you know?" Tseluna said.

"I know," Rory said. "She's a good friend. And she means well. You should be nicer to her."

"Oh, but she's so earnest! She's just too much fun to tease."

26

A FAMILIAR END

(+3 TRALONGS)

CLASS HAD RECONVENED and they were in the middle of a lesson about visualizing magical flows when Tseluna suddenly dug her fingernails into Rory's shoulder.

"That demon is back," she subvocalized as the demon suddenly materialized in the middle of the room. They still had a crude, unfinished form that looked wrong somehow. They began gesticulating and speaking in the demon language. The students all leapt to their feet screaming and backed away.

"What did they say?" Rory asked. He was gaining facility with accessing Tseluna's memories, but with language he could still only recognize words and phrases not fluent speech.

"They say there are a bunch of dragons coming."

"What? They're warning us?"

"Yes. I think you must have been right about them. I will thank them."

Tselune spoke again to the demon that acknowledged her statement and then vanished.

"Wow," Tseluna said, closing her eyes and putting her hands by her temples. "They weren't kidding. There are a lot of dragons arriving."

"But the dragons can't do much," Rory said. "Because there's not much magic here, right?"

"Well, actually," Tseluna admitted. "I learned how to store magic by studying how dragons do it."

"Oh, no," Rory said.

"I could probably defeat a dragon," she continued. "But probably not ten and definitely not a hundred."

"There are a hundred dragons?"

"Oh, no," she said. "There's more than that."

"What about those guys who stopped the tournament? The D-Force … Could they stop the dragons?"

"Oh, they probably could. That's what they're supposed to do, after all: stop trans-dimensional interference. But how are you going to get them here? They don't usually care what happens to these low magic dimensions."

"What would happen if you left the dimension?"

"How would it help if we fled?"

"Not we: you. And then you came back."

"If I left it would … it would break our familiar bond."

"And they would …" Rory prompted.

"They would come to track me down. It's risky."

"But what option do we have? Do it."

Rory and Tseluna had been arguing at breakneck speed and now realized the whole class was staring at them.

"Do it now!" Rory said.

Tseluna opened a dimensional portal. Before she could leave, Rory caught her in his arms and gave her a long, deep kiss to wolf whistles and catcalls from the class. Aimee blushed.

"For luck," he said.

She stepped through. When the dimensional portal closed, Rory felt the familiar bond break and was alone in his head

Relieved, Rory turned his attention back to the dragons. "Can we lure them away?" he wondered.

"Let's try this," Tseluna said and transformed into a gigantic, sleek, winged, black panther. She looked at Rory with her bright yellow eyes. "Climb on. Keep the shield around the school until we're away," she subvocalized. "Then try to keep them back as we fly."

Rory was momentarily stunned by Tseluna's transformation, but then, squealing with excitement, he leapt onto her shoulders and clung to the scruff of her neck.

"Every time I think I can't love you more, you surprise me," he cried, hugging her. "You are the most amazing goddess ever!"

"*Baka!*"

She leapt into the sky and, with tremendous wing beats, lifted up toward the clouds. Rory dedicated himself to maintaining the shield, until the dragons took to flight after them. Tseluna climbed higher and higher. Rory watched as the last of the students departed the rooftop and finally dropped the shield over the school. He then strengthened the shield around the two of them as much as he could.

"At the rate we're using magic, it's a good thing I just refilled my supply," Tseluna subvocalized.

"Should I try to conserve magic?" Rory asked.

"Don't," Tseluna said. "Use it all to buy us time."

Rory wracked his brains for an idea: any idea. He didn't want to throw fireballs with the school below him. Then he had an inspiration. He gathered a vast amount of magic as the dragons closed in.

"Get ready to teleport us about a half mile that way," he said pointing vaguely.

"Roger," she said.

"Now!" Rory said, silently triggering a spell. He felt the shift in the world as Tseluna took them away.

Suddenly, he was looking back at the space they had just occupied that was now filled with a gigantic fireball. The dragons flying at top speed tried to peel off but then the fireball exploded.

A huge shockwave threw the dragons backward and spread an immense cloud of sparks and gledes through the afternoon sky.

Rory looked up and saw another contingent of dragons swarming them from above.

"Dive!" he called to Tseluna. She folded her wings and stooped like a falcon, but the dragons were closing in. Rory held on as tight as he dared and put everything he had into maintaining their shield as the dragons breathed streams of fire and sent clouds of windblades and magic missiles after them.

As they approached the ground, Tseluna extended her wings to slow their fall. They led the dragons on a merry chase for some minutes, dodging among trees and pulling ahead and then having to change direction as the dragons closed off avenues of escape. Eventually, however, the dragons surrounded them and forced them down toward the ground.

"Can you teleport us again?" he subvocalized to Tseluna.

"There are too many of them now, they're blocking me," she said.

The dragons' shields began to bump against their shield and pushed them down. Finally, they hit the ground hard and tumbled. Rory was thrown from Tseluna's back and found himself being held under a dragon's foot. Five dragons were holding Tseluna as she struggled wildly.

"Don't hurt her!" Rory said. "It was me! I'm the one you're after. I was the one who used a trick to win."

"You are in no position to bargain, insect," the dragon said. "If I pushed just a little, I could squash you. We have you and your entire dimension at our mercy. We will make an example of you to demonstrate what happens to anyone who seeks to trifle with mighty dragons!"

As the dragon was speaking, Rory was watching the sky and noticed when a circle of figures appeared high overhead.

"Don't look now," Rory said. "But I think your declaration of victory may be premature."

The dragons started to react but were frozen as transparent crystals formed around them. Their eyes could still move, however, and Rory could see their fury and rage. Then he felt his familiar bond to Tseluna vanish.

Squirming furiously, he managed to get out from under the immobilized dragon and saw that Tseluna was also encased in crystal. He ran to her as the D-force descended, tapping on the dragons one by one, sending them back.

A demon materialized before him. Unlike the crude and unfinished-looking demon, this demon was wearing a colorful set of polished armor and gleamed like a superhero. Rory stood between Tseluna and the demon with his arms outstretched.

"Tseluna is mine!" Rory shouted. "You can't take her."

"THIS ONE VIOLATED THEIR PAROLE," the demon subvocalized. "THEY MUST ACCEPT THE CONSEQUENCES FOR THEIR ACTIONS."

"No!" Rory said. "It was *my* decision. I ordered her as my familiar to break the bond. If you must punish someone, punish me."

Rory felt the demon mind probe him. He closed his eyes and opened himself up wide. When Tseluna had done it, it had been a violent affair, but this was far worse. He felt his mind violated and ransacked by an alien intelligence. He dropped to his knees with the shock and shook his head a few times. Then he heard the demon laughing.

"YOUR SOLUTION IS ACCEPTABLE," the demon said, gestured at him, and dematerialized. In just moments, the dragons and demons were all gone.

Rory looked up. Tseluna had been freed from the crystal and was, again, naked in her human form. And, Rory realized, once again, they both had collars that were joined by a single shining cord. As he felt the familiar bond settle back over him, he walked to her and looked down into her beautiful yellow eyes.

"We did it," he said, reaching out his hand.

"We did it," she echoed, accepting his hand and then, joining in an embrace, they kissed. Rory's class came running out whooping with excitement and caught them.

•　　•　　•

Two weeks later, at sunset, they stood together under the chestnut tree on the town green. Lit by the flickering elemental lights, Rory was wearing a new suit with his mop of hair neatly trimmed. Tseluna wore a daring scarlet dress with a neckline that plunged far beyond the limits of propriety. Rory was backed by Aimee who stood up for him. Tseluna was flanked by Buck with Miri on his shoulder.

Practically the entire town had turned out for the ceremony. The town green was filled from one end to the other to witness the marriage of the heroes.

The Magister convened the ceremony and welcomed the community to celebrate the joining of Rory and Tseluna in matrimony. There was a huge cheer that made Rory blush. He looked over at Tseluna and his heart filled with pride.

The Magister called on Aimee to speak for Rory.

"Tseluna," Aimee said, tears streaming down her face. "I release Rory Soletsa to your care. May you find happiness together."

Then the Magister called on Buck.

"Rory," Buck said with a grin. "I offer Tseluna to you. Treasure her and keep her safe."

Then they took Rory's left hand and Tseluna's right and tied them together with a yellow ribbon. Rory and Tseluna turned to face each other. Rory laced his fingers together with Tseluna and met her eyes.

"Do you, Rory Soletsa, take Tseluna in marriage?" the Magister intoned.

"I do," he said.

"And do you, Tseluna, take Rory Soletsa in marriage?"

"I do."

"I pronounce you married. May you find happiness, health, and prosperity together."

The whole town erupted in cheers. Rory's dad ran up and hugged them both, trying not to cry. Rory's aunt and uncle and cousins cheered them. Rory's grandfather shook Rory's hand while his grandmother hugged Tseluna.

"Thank you," she whispered to Tseluna. "Thank you for keeping my precious boy safe."

"He is the one who kept me safe," Tseluna replied, hugging her back.

A buffet had been set up to the side and there was music. Rory and Tseluna took the ceremonial first dance and then turned the dancing over to others. They stayed for a while greeting well-wishers, but it quickly became tedious.

"Is it time, my goddess?" Rory asked.

"I'm ready, *Baka*," Tseluna said. She quietly opened a portal and they stepped through to the sea coast below Tseluna's *onsen*, ready for their honeymoon and what would come next.

OMAKE

ABOUT TWENTY TRALONGS before the Familiar Tournament, and after another long day of training, Rory fell asleep promptly after Tseluna compelled him to go TO bed. He was always angling for ways to stay up a little later, but he'd been training hard and really needed the sleep.

Tseluna lay next to him on the bed and brushed his unruly hair from his face. As a demon, she didn't need to sleep. She enjoyed looking at the face of her familiar while he slept, and she twirled a lock of his hair around her finger. His face, so lively when he was awake, was relaxed and peaceful; his breathing was slow and even.

After a few minutes, she noticed a catch in his breathing and saw his eyes begin to dart back and forth underneath his eyelids. From long experience with people, she knew this meant that he was starting to dream. Using the familiar bond, she closed her eyes and slipped into his dreaming mind.

She found herself standing in a freshly plowed field where Rory sat on the ground rowing with a pair of oars while birds wheeled overhead making raucous cries.

"Where are you going?" she asked.

"The miner said the alcohol was too long," he mumbled. "I'm going to catch a rock in the water barrel."

Tseluna snorted with laughter. When she had first encountered people, she had discovered the weird phenomenon of dreaming but, after discovering that it didn't really mean anything, she hadn't bothered to enter anyone's dreams in millions of tralongs. But she had to admit that Rory really was something special.

She found herself genuinely hoping to win the tournament so that he might survive. She had considered just pulling him out. But, having made the commitment, it was too hard to back out now. And if she wasn't training him for the tournament, what were they even doing? No, she would just have to train him as best she could and then they would have to take their chances in the tournament. There was always next year ...

A kind of mist sprang up in the field and grew thicker until everything was whited out. Then the mist faded away and they were in a different setting. Now they were in a crowded festival, except the people were all faceless. Their faces were just pale, featureless ovals.

"Treble force leaves branches," Rory mumbled, pointing vaguely. "Where dogs fly bridge traffic."

"You're not making any sense, Sugar," she said. "Maybe this will help!"

Tseluna took his face between her hands. His eyes were vacant and uncomprehending. She pressed her mouth to his and thrust her rough tongue into his mouth. After a moment, his eyes came into focus, and he seized her and kissed her back passionately as the scene changed again.

Tseluna found herself standing on the stairs of a golden throne where Rory was seated. He was wearing a tiger skin belted around him and was holding a unsheathed sword across his lap. His eyes blazed with fervor. The room was dim, lit by flickering torchlight.

"Dance for me!" he called out and clapped his hands. Musicians began to play and struck up a tune with drums and a heavy bass line.

Tseluna looked down and saw that she was wearing a costume of diaphanous silks and realized she was wearing a collar around her neck with a shining cord that Rory was holding in his fist.

"Wait," she said. "How did …"

"Dance!" Rory bellowed, standing.

"Yes, Master," she said with a wink. She backed down the steps, struck a pose with her arms raised over her head, and then began to dance. She had studied kabuki, ballet, modern dance, and belly dancing over her time among people, and her performance drew from all four traditions. Rory seated himself upon the throne, leaned forward, and watched her avidly as she pirouetted and turned to the music. He devoured her with his gaze. She felt his eyes on her as she gyrated to the music.

After two or three minutes, he stood suddenly and bellowed again, "Bring in the prisoner!" The music trailed off and Tseluna stopped and turned to look at the door. Two faceless guards dragged in a figure in chains. It was Aimee. She was wearing a thin nightgown and had an ordinary collar that was linked with chains to manacles binding her wrists.

"What's going on? Where am I? What's happening?" she asked, looking around in panic.

"You're in Rory's dream," Tseluna explained.

"What?" Aimee said.

"Sorry," Tseluna said, then gestured at herself. "I came to see what he was dreaming about and look what happened to me."

"Silence!" Rory bellowed. "I will have silence!"

"Yes, Master," Tseluna said, kneeling down before him and performing an obeisance.

"That's better," Rory said, mollified, taking his seat. "Now you must please me with your dancing or the prisoner will be punished."

"What?" Aimee said, again.

"I will do my best, Master," Tseluna said and, coming to her feet, she struck the same pose. Rory clapped his hands and the music started up once more. This time, Tseluna performed a purely belly-dancing routine that she knew from past experience was particularly popular with the boys. Her bare feet slapped the floor as she twisted, turned, and undulated under Rory's all-consuming gaze.

Aimee was also mesmerized watching her perform. Tseluna spun as the music tempo increased and then she cast off the diaphanous silks and danced in the nude. She watched Rory's gleaming eyes follow her across the floor. Aimee blushed and looked down. Then she looked up, her eyes irresistibly drawn to the erotic vision before her.

The music got faster and faster as Tseluna whirled and spun and then finally came to a crashing end. Tseluna stood still with the backs of her wrists touching over her head as she panted, damp with perspiration, her chest heaving. Rory stood and came down the stairs. He grabbed her roughly and spun her around to face him. He ran his thumb over her lips and then pressed his mouth to hers. Then he turned to the guards.

"Punish the prisoner!"

"What?" Aimee said, yet again. The guards split the nightgown Aimee was wearing to expose her back and one of them uncoiled a whip and snapped it with a loud crack. Aimee trembled in fear.

"Wait, Master," Tseluna said, pulling at Rory's tiger skin.

"Silence!" Rory said. "Guards! Now!"

The guard drew back his arm and Aimee braced herself for the first stroke of the whip when the scenery changed again.

Aimee looked around, bewildered. Now she was standing in a kitchen wearing a gingham apron over her nightgown when Rory came in wearing a ruffled shirt and tie, with the tie loosened.

"I'm home from work, dear!" he said, putting his arms around Aimee. She looked up at him with surprise. He bent down and kissed her familiarly on the mouth, leaving her speechless with shock.

"How's our little girl?" he continued.

"What?" Aimee said, now for the fourth time. She looked over and saw a small Black toddler run into the room and grab her leg.

"Mommy!" Tseluna squealed.

"No, no, no!" Aimee said. "This is too weird."

"I think Sunny needs her nummies," Rory said, with a strange fey affect. He scooped up Tseluna and led Aimee over to a comfortable chair, seated her, and handed Tseluna to her.

"What are you talking about?" Aimee said. Tseluna pulled at her shirt and began to root for her nipple.

"Oh, no!" Aimee said. "No! Not that! You won't get anything anyway."

"Try, Mommy!" Tseluna said. "Try!"

"Whose side are you on?" she asked.

"Just relax," Tseluna whispered. "This isn't really happening. It's just a dream."

"Does he always have such weird dreams?"

"Oh, you should see his fantasies!"

"Ugh!" Aimee said. "Are they weirder than this?"

Tseluna just rolled her eyes.

"Does he really think of you—of me!—like this?"

Rory was carrying on an incomprehensible conversation with himself, "Next week, the topsoil is Blink four chicken."

"No," Tseluna whispered to Aimee. "This has nothing to do with what Rory actually thinks. Not really. This is a dream. It's just an artifact of how your monkey brains work and none of it actually means anything. It was probably just as likely for me to end up as the mommy."

"Really?"

"Yep—except then you would have been able to actually get something," Tseluna purred with a wink.

Aimee just stared at her with a withering look of morbid disgust.

"Am I actually really even here, though?" Aimee asked. "Are you sure *I'm* not just dreaming? Why am I asking you?"

"I don't think you're just dreaming. I think you really are here," Tseluna said. "I've been keeping an eye on you to make sure you didn't talk, and I think that's how you got drawn into Rory's dream too."

"Wendy said cloud stone guildhall," Rory continued. Aimee's ears perked up.

"Who's Wendy?" Aimee asked, naturally curious about any girls whom Rory might be involved with.

Tseluna shrugged.

"How do we get out of his dream?"

"His dream won't last very long," Tseluna said. "Just enjoy it while you can."

As if responding to her statement, the mist moved back in and then drained away, leaving Rory standing in the middle of an arena. Tseluna stood behind him while Aimee was up in the stands surrounded by a restive crowd. Facing Rory was a gigantic dragon. It saw Rory and its pupils constricted when it recognized him.

Tseluna similarly recognized instantly that it was the dragon from the qualifying round. And she feared, as with Aimee, somehow the actual dragon had been drawn into his dream. If so, this was bad. Very, very bad.

"It's *you!*" the dragon bellowed. "How dare you disturb my slumber!"

"Oh, hey, look! It's that *idiot* dragon!" Rory snorted.

Tseluna cringed and wanted to cover her face. Even if she were to fight a dragon herself, it would be a close thing with nearly even odds. Moreover, everyone knew it was madness to mock a dragon because they were so prideful. Once they lost their temper, there was no way to ever talk them back down.

The dragon roared with rage and breathed out a huge blast of fire. Aimee drew her breath in and covered her eyes with her hands, peeking out only between her fingers. Rory casually raised his shield against the fire. The flame passed over him without harm.

"Don't look now, but your shoe's untied!" Rory called, chuckling. Raising his hand, he produced a giant lightning strike with a brilliant flash and deafening bang, but the dragon had raised a shield too. They circled one another in the arena, looking for a weakness. Tseluna blanched. She tried to contact Rory via the familiar bond, but in Rory's dream it was reversed and didn't work right.

"Your fly is open!" Rory snickered, now openly laughing at the dragon. Tseluna cast about desperately for what she could do to avert this catastrophe. Then she had an idea.

"Aimee!" Tseluna called. "You've got to wake him up!"

"How can I do that from here?"

Tseluna gestured at her, and Aimee felt a strange twist in her equilibrium. Suddenly she was in two places at once: she was still in the stadium, but she was also standing in her nightgown in Rory's bedroom. Her head felt really weird as she had double vision bouncing back and forth between the two environments. In the bedroom, Rory and Tseluna were tangled together, seemingly asleep and naked on his bed.

"Disgusting!" Aimee said, averting her eyes.

She grabbed Rory's shoulder and shook him. He was unresponsive.

"Hurry!" Tseluna called, as bestial roars sounded in the background intermixed with Rory's hysterical, unhinged laughter. "Live dragons are not something to laugh at!"

Aimee looked down at his peacefully sleeping face.

"C'mon, Sleepy Princess!" she said, shaking him again. She blushed when she realized what she'd said. Then she shrugged and, bending over, she kissed him full on the lips. She kissed him gently at first, then pressed harder and pushed her tongue into his mouth. She felt him respond to her, then his eyes popped open and came into focus.

"Aimee!" he sputtered, frantically trying to pull the covers over himself. But Tseluna was lying on top of them. She rubbed her eyes and grinned at Aimee.

"Well done!" she said.

Aimee backed slowly away, her eyes wide. She pointed her finger at Rory.

"This never happened," she said, menacingly. "We will never speak of this!" Then she realized she was only wearing a nightgown.

"Wait! How am I going to get home?" she squeaked.

Tseluna gestured peremptorily and Aimee vanished. Then Tseluna looked at Rory, who had his hands over his mouth.

"Smooth ..." he mused. "So smooooooth ..."

ABOUT THE AUTHOR

Steven D. Brewer has been a fan of science fiction and fantasy stories for as long as he can remember. He still remembers getting scolded for not reading chapter books in fourth grade because he was avidly consuming *The Hobbit* late at night, by flashlight under his covers. And he probably got his copy from his older brother and most important mentor. Steven currently teaches scientific writing at the University of Massachusetts Amherst. He lives in Amherst, Massachusetts with his extended family.

ALSO BY THE AUTHOR

BETTER ANGELS: TOUR DE FORCE
FROM THE TRUCK STOP AT THE CENTER OF THE GALAXY
by Steven D. Brewer

The Better Angels. Entertainment. Music and Dancing. And Rescues!

REVIN'S HEART
by Steven D. Brewer

A young man falls in with airship pirates ... and discovers how to follow his heart.

Available from Water Dragon Publishing in
hardcover, trade paperback, and digital editions
waterdragonpublishing.com